Scorched Earth

Stephen Monaco

For my wife and kids. Thank you for all the love and support you've given me while I chased my dream.

Contents

4

Chapter 1

Shayna Coldrake eased the truck around to the back side of a two-story house, watching for any sign of life. Nothing. For a few minutes, she sat with the truck in gear in case she needed to flee. Or run somebody down. Icicles of jagged glass served as windows, and the backdoor lay on the ground outside. Both of which were good signs that the home's occupants were dead and no one else had decided to move in.

She pulled down the mirror and checked her disguise, a curly black wig, wide-brimmed hat, and oversized sunglasses. She'd never really considered it much of a disguise, but today it struck her how much younger she looked by covering up the dark circles under her damaged eyes and the ever-growing patch of gray where her hair parted. It easily took off ten years.

Her younger looking reflection sent pangs of nostalgia rushing through her. Granted, she and the boys were better off than most people, but she would give almost anything to go back to her life before Impact when she had family, friends, and a good job. She thought about her friends, her book club, and even the old biddies at the church that liked to gossip about Allen's drinking and dalliances. She'd even go back to the drunken beatings if it meant she'd get the rest of her life back. If it meant she got to wear makeup again. If she got to shop for clothes, shoes, and purses with a credit card, instead of trading vegetables and seeds for meat and gasoline.

Seeing the sack of vegetables and little bag of seeds on the seat next to her caused tears to threaten for the third time in the last few hours. This was her life. And she hated it. She took a last glance at the house to make sure she was alone, then allowed herself a few minutes to let go. The tears came like a spring downpour; sobs wracked her body. Between the sobs she cursed. She cursed the Impact, she cursed living every day in fear, and she cursed the loneliness. Once the tears slowed, she pulled the pistol out of the sack and got out of the truck.

The morning air was thick and acrid. Since she left the homestead, the dark clouds had thickened. A storm was brewing. Morning storms usually led to some of the hottest and most miserable days, and today might be setting up to be a doozy.

Once the acidic rain sickened everything it touched, the sun would come out and scorch it. If it weren't for Allen's obsessive preparation, the family probably would've starved like so many others during the winter that followed Impact. She used to scoff at the money he spent building the greenhouse, digging wells, and installing generators. He may not have been a great husband, but his preparation was the reason the boys were alive, and for that she was grateful.

Yellowish weeds crunched under her feet as she moved to the opening where the backdoor used to hang. With the gun pressed against her chest, she leaned and peered around the jamb. A little pink windbreaker hung on a hook, and a pair of small rain boots sat below it, one lying on its side. The girl who used to wear them couldn't have been more than a few years old. Those poor parents. How horrible that must have been for them. She said a silent prayer that she wouldn't live to see a day where she had to watch one of her boys die. A tear strolled down her cheek.

She stepped through the doorway and into the kitchen. The window sill was squishy from rot; the wall and the sink below it teemed with black mold. The refrigerator hung open and empty. She stepped over the collapsed remains of a dead rat on her way to the living room. Wallpaper hung, half-peeled, in long strips like giant fingers reaching out of the wall. Bookshelves around the fireplace had been ransacked. The couch was tipped over on its front. She bent and picked up a book, Stephen King's *The Stand*.

"How appropriate," she said.

Something moved on the other side of the room.

Frozen, she listened for it again but didn't think she'd be able to hear anything over her pounding heart. It came from behind, or under, the couch. She held the gun in front of her, but her trembling hands moved it all around. Nothing had better come out of there too fast because her aim would be poor.

"Don't think I won't put a bullet in you right now!" she said.

"Don't... pl... pl...please don't," said a deep voice from under the couch.

"Come outta there. I wanna see your hands. Don't try anything or I'll fill ya with lead."

"D... D...Don... Don't shoot m... me, 'kay?"

Two hands, caked with dirt but empty, poked out from the end of the couch. A few grunts and moans led to arms, and then a head slinking out from the tent-like opening. His eyes were blue. Brilliant blue. His face was dirty, and his head had been shaved, but the hair was starting to grow back. He looked young, maybe twenty, probably younger. Those eyes, though. So bright, but so full of fear. The kid reminded her of Frank, her oldest son.

"Ca... Can you hel... hel... help me? Please... don... don't turn me in?"

"Turn you in?"

"To th... the Rav... Rav... Raven...s. I don't wan... na go ba...back."

She used one hand to help drag the boy out from under the couch, then pointed the gun at him as he stood up. He held his hands out to his sides, palms facing the ceiling. Beyond the eyes, he didn't look much like Frank. He was tall like Frank but much less bulky, scrawny even. Frank had a full beard; this kid had a heavy stubble, like he'd gone several days without shaving. But she couldn't stop looking at those blue eyes and seeing her son. So frightened. So harmless looking.

Though, Frank wasn't totally harmless. He'd beaten Allen to death six months ago. She was sure Frank hadn't meant to; he just didn't understand his own strength. Frank didn't understand a lot, and he often looked at her with the same helpless, scared eyes that this kid had.

"Why do the Ravens want you?"

"I ran aw... aw... away from the far...farm. Ple... please don't ma... make me go back."

"The farm?"

The kid winced, and his eyes focused on the gun as if he was thinking whether or not he could grab it before she shot him.

"Don't even think about it, kid," Shayna warned. "Now what farm did you run away from and why are the Ravens after you?" She bounced the business end of the pistol up and down to make it seem like the shaking was intentional and not because of her hands trembling.

He must've believed it because he refocused on her and pointed at the back of his neck before moving back to his original position. "Here."

She motioned with the gun for him to turn around. His blue eyes filled with tears as he nodded and turned. Shayna gasped. No less than six gaping red slashes crisscrossed his back. A few scars were an angry shade of pink against his pale skin, and an eggplant-colored bruise along his ribcage had started to turn greenish at the edges. On the back of his neck was a tattoo that read: Property of Farm 1256.

"Did the Ravens do this to you?" she said.

She read his neck again to be sure. Property of Farm 1256. Property? Was he a slave? Her face reddened, and she chastised herself for being so naïve about how uncivilized civilization had become since Impact. She knew of big farming operations to the south where teenage boys worked, but she thought the boys were working for wages, not as slaves.

It shouldn't have surprised her, but living out on the homestead had insulated her from some of the atrocities in the towns. Allen had always wanted her and the boys as far away from all of it as they could be, and before he died, she was more than happy to oblige. If she didn't see it, it was easier to pretend it wasn't real.

Since his death, she'd attempted to adapt, but her quick trips to the markets to trade didn't allow her time to find out what else was happening in the world. She vowed to change that. She *needed* to change that. How scary that boys around her sons' ages were being enslaved!

He turned around and faced her, his arms still out, palms up. His blue eyes begged for help. "They so... sold me to the f... fa... farm."

She lowered the gun to her side. "What's your name?"

He blinked and brushed his eye with the back of his hand. "G... G...Gordon."

"How old are you, Gordon?"

"Eightte..teen."

She motioned with her gun hand; Gordon winced and jumped backward, his arms covering crossing in front of him. She felt another pang of shame. After years of Allen's drunken abuse, she often noticed herself wincing if someone made a sudden movement. It didn't matter if it was one of the boys or one of her friends, sudden movements triggered the flight reflex. She'd just done the same to this boy.

"Sorry. I was just gonna tell you to put your hands down. I'm not going to hurt you... or tell the Ravens about you. Just relax."

He eased his hands down to his side but still looked nervous.

"Are you hungry?"

He nodded.

"Stay here. I've got a little food I'll get for you."

She hurried to the truck and got the bag of vegetables and the seeds and went back in the house. Her stomach flip-flopped as she walked past the little pink windbreaker and rain boots again. Gordon had put the couch back to its normal position and was sitting on it. Her gut flopped again when she saw those eyes. Something about them gnawed at her. It wasn't just that they reminded her of Frank; it was something just beyond her ability to verbalize. Something scary. Something tragic.

She rummaged through the bag and handed Gordon a couple of carrots and three small potatoes. "It's not much, but it's something to get a little food in you." She bit into a carrot, and he followed her lead. "Do you have any family?"

He shook his head. "They all di...died in the w... w... winter." He nibbled at the carrot like he was trying to make it last as long as possible.

"My husband died from the cold, too." It was a lie, but she wanted to make the kid feel comfortable. She didn't know why she thought saying that would help him, but she said it anyway. "I have two sons, both close to your age."

"They d... didn't d... die?"

She shook her head and gazed at the carrot in her hand.

"What are their na... na...names?"

"Frank and Cain," she said without thinking. She immediately chastised herself for being so careless. She didn't know this kid. She trusted very few people in town; only a couple knew the boys even existed or about the greenhouse. But here she was freely sharing information with a total stranger.

"Cain? Skinny C... Cain?"

Her gut lurched into her throat. Skinny Cain is what Frank used to call his younger brother. She tried to steady her voice. "Might not be the same Cain," she said.

"B... black hair, about this l... l... long"--he motioned to just above his shoulders--"big sc... scar on h... his arm."

The last one was the clincher. Cain had a scar that ran from his elbow to the back of his hand from a bike wreck he'd had when he was ten. He and one of his friends had built a ramp from a piece of corrugated metal and convinced Frank to lie underneath it while they jumped over him on their bikes. The friend made it over okay, but Cain thought he was going to land on his brother so reared back, let go, and tried to launch the bike forward with his legs. The bike tumbled across the ground a few feet past Frank, but Cain came down on the edge of the metal sheet, slicing his arm open. If Gordon knew the scar, that meant he knew Cain.

"He says I re... remind him of his br... brother, Big D... Dummy. But I'm not du... dumb I just st... st... stut... stutter when I get scared."

Her stomach lurched again. She hated Cain using that name. When the boys were little, it was ordinary sibling teasing, but as he got older, Cain's resentment of his brother seemed to get more venomous, especially after Allen died. She'd always imagined the boys being close, and after Impact, she prayed that Cain would learn to return Frank's affection. Hearing Gordon say that name dealt that dream a significant blow.

"How do you know Cain?" she said, trying to compose herself.

"He's my f... friend. He helped me after m... my fa... family died. He brought me f... f... food and helped me hide from the R... Ravens."

"Helped you hide?"

"Yeah. S... So I wouldn't ha...ha... have to register with the Ra... Ravens. Cain said that h... he would hel... help me 'cause when you're nice to p... pe... pe... people, they'll be n... nice to you." His face dropped and tears perched on his eyes again.

Shayna wished Cain's outlook applied to his older brother. Frank adored Cain but often got nothing but vitriol in return. Frank was nice, but Cain sure wasn't nice back.

"If Cain helped you hide, how did you end up at the farms?"

Gordon sighed and looked up from the carrot that he'd been nibbling on. "They f... found me hid... hiding in a van. C... C... Cain said to stay there for two d... days, and he'd come back. They found me, ti... tied me up, and put me in the back of a tr... tr... truck. I saw Cain when th... they were taking me away. He was cr... cr... cr--"

Tears welled up in Gordon's eyes again. Shayna scooted closer and put her hand on his arm. He didn't pull away. For a second, she felt like she was comforting Frank. Gordon looked up, then reached over and hugged her. She let him.

"Cain was crying when you got caught?" she finally said, easing herself away from Gordon's embrace. That thought gave her a little hope for Cain. He'd always maintained a certain emotional distance from both her and Frank, but since Allen's death, it was more of an outright wall. During these last months, at best he seemed indifferent toward them, at worst, downright hostile. That's when he was even home, which lately, wasn't all that often. The idea that he could feel emotion toward a stranger, especially one reminded him of Frank, made her feel a little better.

"Yeah."

"When was this?" she asked but was fairly sure she knew the answer. There were a few days last month that Cain was in an exceptionally bad mood. He only came out of his room to do his chores. The rest of the time, he laid on his mattress tossing an old baseball up and catching it. At the time she thought he was missing life before Impact, but now she knew better. Hope continued to build inside her.

"About a mo... month ago."

She couldn't stop the smile that ran across her face.

Hope lived.

"How'd you escape?"

"They t... told everyone that the Ravens would k... k... kill our family if we tried to run away. One b... boy said that his family was all dead anyway, like mine, so he was gon... gon... gonna run. He ran, but they caught him. I think t... th... they killed him. I watched the g... guards and knew what t... time they changed shifts and when the n... new patrol would get to us. I ran and was g... gone by the time the patrol got there. Cain taught me how to st... study the patrols when he was hel... helping me hide. Will y... y... you tell him that I did it, and it worked?"

She smiled. "Why don't you come home with me and tell him yourself?"

Chapter 2

Shayna walked the mile toward town a little quicker than normal. It was too risky to bring Gordon to town with her, so she left him hiding behind the couch. She hoped that bringing Gordon to Cain would help thaw her relationship with her youngest son. She didn't know if Cain blamed her for Allen's death or if he just felt the responsibility of being the man of the house since his older brother wasn't capable of that responsibility. Whatever it was, she wanted to fix it, and Gordon might be a step toward that.

Up ahead she could start to see that shape of the buildings that made up the town of Lake Brenton. Before Impact, it was a bustling tourist trap. The lake itself hadn't always been so commercial, but as its reputation as a must-go destination for the Midwest grew, little burgs sprouted up all around it, filled with restaurants, bars, and all sorts of touristy knick-knacks people could purchase to memorialize their vacation. Main Street in Lake Brenton was the oldest, biggest, and most popular. She remembered bringing the boys when they were young to ride the little roller coaster ride that sat next to the pier. Cain wanted to go; Frank didn't but went along because he didn't want Cain to have to ride alone. He held his little brother's hand the whole time.

She cherished that memory, seeing her boys laughing and giggling and looking out for each other.

Now, the roller coaster was mostly gone; a few posts still stood, and some remnants of track lay scattered on the ground, but most of it had long since been scavenged. Main Street, which once hosted reveling vacationers, now was a line of mostly empty storefronts and boarded-up windows. In front of them were makeshift stands, some crudely constructed from wood, others nothing more than pop-up canopies and a couple of card tables. All revelry was long gone, replaced by solemn bartering for items essential for life.

The clouds grew darker across the still lake. The trees on the far side were brighter, greener, like they were thankful for a brief respite from the heat of the blazing sun. But she knew that soon enough the sun would appear, leaving a trail of scorched earth in its wake.

Screams from the market echoed down the road, jolting her from her thoughts. She adjusted her bag across her chest and put her right hand into it, wrapping her fingers around the cool steel of the gun. More screams. She hurried toward the faded marquee that spanned the road, marking the entrance to town. Once lit by colorful neon lights, it used to read: Lake Brenton, the Happiest Place in the Midwest. Now it was broken and dark, an ominous reminder of how much had changed. The screams were another reminder.

Three men in black jackets had hold of a man's arms and were dragging him out from one of the stands. A woman, probably his wife, clung to his back; her screams tore through the air. "Noooooo!" she cried. A fourth man pulled her away and held her, her throat cradled in his arm. She scratched and kicked at the man, but he tightened his hold around her throat until she quit resisting.

Shayna stood just under the marquee with her hand still touching the gun in her bag. The man restraining the wife wrestled around with her a little until his back was toward Shayna. The back of his jacket was emblazoned with a black bird, talons exposed, swooping downward. The Ravens. Her little handgun wouldn't do her much good against the firepower they had. She slipped her hand out of her bag and slid her hat lower in the front. It was better to go unnoticed.

About thirty people stopped and watched the drama on the old Main Street. Others looked like they were trying to busy themselves, but she noticed their eyes occasionally drifting toward the unfolding scene. About a dozen stands away, a stand owner with long gray hair and a close-cropped beard gave her a long look before waving another customer over. She'd been noticed. She turned away and began examining the produce selection at the nearest stand.

"David Benoit, are you part of an organized sedition movement?"

"No! He's not!" the woman said, her face turned skyward and her fists clenched.

"Beth, let me talk," he said to the woman, then turned back to the big Raven. "No, I'm not part of any movement. I'm just a merchant trying to take care of my family. I've paid my tithe to you guys. I'll give more. I can--"

"Have you harbored fugitives?"

"Fugitives? No!"

Shayna picked up a cucumber and put it back down. The last thing she needed was more vegetables, but she wanted to look interested. Finally, she nodded at the stand owner and moved toward the next one.

The man that had been dragged out of his stand was in the street with his hands tied behind his back. The Ravens had tossed a rope over his stand's canopy support beam. Each time they pulled the rope, it forced his arms higher behind his back. His face glowed red, and his eyes bulged. He gritted his teeth. His wife sobbed. She tried to push free from the hold the man in black had on her, but she didn't have the strength. She cried harder.

Shayna looked away and checked out the offerings at the next stand. Clothes for little girls and dolls, she had no use for that so kept moving. Looking around, she noticed the gray-haired shop owner was looking at her again. This time he didn't avert his gaze; she felt its weight. His hair was thick, unkempt, and hung below his shoulders. He wore a long-sleeve black shirt and unbuttoned it a few buttons exposing a white t-shirt with a crudely-drawn upside-down American flag. He nodded once, then rebuttoned the shirt. His eyes were fierce. They scared her. She reminded herself that she was disguised but could feel the cold rush of panic in her gut. She shivered and ducked under the canopy at the next stand.

Another voice spoke from the street. Shayna didn't look but was sure it wasn't one of the original players. "I beg to differ, David. Not only have you harbored fugitives, you've aided Skinny Cain"--the cold hand of panic closed around Shayna's gut and tugged, nearly causing her to double over--"in helping seventeen-year-olds avoid their evaluation with the Ravens. In fact, your son is seventeen and remains unreported and unevaluated."

Shayna struggled to steady her breathing. *'I can't let them see me panic. Calm down!'* she told herself. She blew out a long breath, then asked the stand owner to see a few cuts of pork. While he turned to pull them out, she blew out a couple more breaths. *Cain! The Ravens mentioned Cain! Stay calm, or someone will notice.* She glanced toward the gray-haired man's stand. He was looking her direction! The invisible cold hand gripped her again.

"I've got these cuts, not exactly pre-Impact pork chops but you'll get full enough. Four of 'em will cost you about a third of a pound of seeds. Or we might be able to work something out in trade," he said with a slimy leer etched on his face.

It took a second for the disgusting offer to sink in. Shayna barely registered what he was saying; she was trying to focus on the street without being obvious about it. She couldn't afford to attract the attention to her that telling him off would bring, so she opted to pretend she hadn't heard him and try to overhear the other discussion.

Beth screamed through her choked sobs, "Paul, you son of a--"

"David, one of your peers has leveled a serious charge against you. He's accused you of treason. That's a death sentence if I find you guilty."

Shayna turned quickly to see who was speaking. It was the largest of the Ravens. He wore glasses and had short hair. His eyes were glazed and milky with damage from the acid rain. Other than his size, he didn't look threatening. But the others deferred to him, so she knew he must have a nasty streak that wasn't obvious by looking at him.

"So what do you think? Third of a pound? Little something else?" the stand owner asked.

"I've got cucumbers, a few tomatoes, and a couple of carrots. Total about four pounds of produce."

He shook his head. "I don't need produce. I gotta have seeds for this pork."

"I don't know. I need to get and only have about a half pound of seeds. Ol' Man McDonald will want seeds for the gas," Shayna said, watching the shop owner for some sort of tell. Her dad taught her long ago to always look for the tell to know what someone was really thinking, an eye twitch, a quick glance to the side, or a nearly imperceptible smirk. This guy either wasn't giving it up or she was missing it. She was afraid it was the latter because all she saw was a despicable pig of a man. It was hard to be revolted by him and try to get a read on him and still listen to the talk in the street at the same time.

"Let me think about it for a little bit." She adjusted her hat and turned to watch the street.

They winched David's arms higher. One of his shoulders popped. He screamed. "He's... lying!" he managed to get out between wails of agony.

The leader nodded, and the one with the rope tugged again. David's arms stretched higher. Another pop. Another scream, this one more primal and terrifying than the last. Beth screamed and cried too.

"You aren't convincing me, David," the big man said.

"Paul! Why are you lying?" Beth said. "You were supposed to be his friend. Our friend!"

"Tell me the truth, David. Do you have an unreported seventeen-year-old son?" the boss Raven said, bending over, so his face was perfectly even with David's.

David's face glowed red. He blew out through gritted teeth, sending spittle into the air and a little running down his chin. The rope winched his arms higher behind his back. They were almost level with his head. He roared again.

"Beth, you know damn well that I'm not lying," Paul said. "Just admit it. Why do you get to protect D.J. when I had to send Carter to be evaluated? They were classmates... and friends. Carter got sent to the farms. Who knows if he'll ever come back from that hellhole. But D.J. is nice and safe in your house. Not exactly fair, is it? Plus, I've personally seen David dealing with Skinny Cain."

"Skinny Cain... is... just... a kid. Not a... traitor." David said through his gritted teeth.

Shayna's adrenaline surged again. *No! Not Cain! Quit saying his name!*

More people had gathered in the street and were watching. Those who were feigning disinterest earlier gave up their acts. Shayna scanned the crowd for a way to slip through without attracting much attention. The gray-haired man was looking her way again. He motioned for her to come toward him and tapped his chest. She pretended not to see. Probably another one like the last guy she'd encountered.

One of the Ravens leaned in and whispered something to the leader.

Beth started kicking at her captor again. One kick landed on his shin, causing his grip to loosen briefly. It was enough to give her space to wrench herself out from under his arm. She sprinted forward, grabbed the rope attached to her husband's arms, and pulled it down. The Raven holding it hadn't processed yet what was happening, so the rope slipped out of his hands. David and his wife both fell to the ground.

"Stay away from him!" she yelled, scrambling to her knees and holding a hand up toward the Ravens. "He's a good man! My family needs him."

"Go search their house if you're inclined to believe her. You'll find the kid there," Paul said, stepping toward the head Raven.

"Who is this Skinny Cain?" the leader said.

"He's just a kid," David said, sitting upright with help from his wife. "A scavenger. He scrounges up car parts for me. Sometimes whole cars. Family don't have much, and he's kind of forced to be the man of the house since his dad died. He's a good kid."

"Where's he live?"

"I don't know. Outside of town somewhere, but I don't know him all that well. I deal in spare parts. He's one of my suppliers. That's all."

The bigger Raven paused like he was thinking and studied his captive. The other men eyed him as if expecting orders.

Okay, stay calm. The Raven guy doesn't know who Cain is. He's not doing anything illegal. Just scavenging car parts. Nothing illegal. He's safe.

And then she remembered Gordon.

The invisible hand grabbed her insides and wouldn't let go. The panic rolled through her. She succumbed and doubled over, trying not to throw up the carrot she'd eaten with Gordon. Her hat fell off and blew to the front of the crowd next to David and his wife, but she caught the wig before it moved out of place. A woman next to her touched her back and asked if she was okay. She tried to answer, but no sound would come out. She nodded.

She felt the weight of the gray-haired man's eyes on her again. Without coming fully upright, she stumbled to the front, grabbed her hat, and put it back on, pulling it low in the front. No one paid much attention to her. Except for that one stand owner. She looked; he was still watching.

"Well somebody is lying," the leader said.

"Skinny Cain helps the resistance smuggle boys out away from Raven territory so they can avoid the evaluation," Paul said. "He trades scavenged parts for food and supplies to give the boys as he moves them from one safe house to the next."

Oh my God. Gordon wasn't the only one Cain hid.

"Really? You seem to know an awful lot about this. How do you know so much? And if you knew all this, why is this the first we're hearing about it?" The Raven stalked toward Paul. "Are these people your friends?" He nodded toward David and his wife.

Paul nodded. "They were until they didn't send D.J. for his evaluation. "Why'd I have to lose my son and not them?"

The big man licked his lips and motioned to his men. "I hate traitors. I really do. Hard to maintain a sense of civilization if folks don't obey the law. Civilization is what separates us from animals" He walked back and forth in front of David and Beth, motioning to the crowd like a politician at a campaign rally. He made eye contact with as many in the crowd as he could. "The novel, *Lord of the Flies,* warns us about how unstable a society without law becomes. Since the Impact, we've all struggled to build a civilization from the ground up. None of us want to go back to the anarchy after our government collapsed. Our worst nightmares were realized during those days. We were tested. The challenge was hard, but we prevailed!"

He motioned to the crowd to applaud. A few people exchanged nervous glances then clapped quietly; a few more followed. David and Beth had started to scoot toward the curb. One of the Ravens stepped up behind them and blocked their progress.

"We prevailed! And we rebuilt this town into a thriving society. But if we have people ignoring laws, undermining authority, and poisoning the thoughts of others, our society will suffer. People must believe, without hesitation, in what we're trying to accomplish here. If you aren't trying to make our society better, you're just a poser. I hate traitors, but I hate posers almost as much. Hang all three of them! Hang 'em from the marquee--"

"I was loyal," Paul yelled.

A gasp rolled through the crowd. Beth screamed. Ravens grabbed her and David and jerked them to their feet.

The leader shook his head. "No. No, you didn't. You turned in people that were you called your friends. You didn't turn on them out of a sense of civic pride or duty. You turned on them out of petty jealousy. You said so yourself. Doing the right thing for the wrong reasons is just as bad as doing the wrong thing. You're a poser!"

Paul stared straight ahead; his mouth gaped, and his eyes grew wider by the second as the understanding of his fate made its way through his nervous system. He turned and tried to run, but was tackled by one of the Ravens and pulled to his feet; blood poured from his nose. The head Raven stepped forward and watched Paul's blood drip into dark lines on the ground. Then in one fluid motion, he pulled the club from his belt and brought it to bear on Paul's right hip. Paul screamed. The crowd eased back.

The Raven spun the baton in his hand. He acted like he was going to swing it at Paul again but stopped short. "You aren't even worth hitting again. Let the other two watch him get strung up. Their disloyalty was the beginning of all this. They can repent while they watch. And search their house. If you find this D.J. there, hang him too." He started to walk away then paused before speaking to the gathered crowd. "Anyone that brings this Skinny Cain to me alive will be rewarded with a steer and a cow. Make sure that gets around. I want him, and I want him alive."

A steer and a cow?! That was the equivalent of several hundred thousand dollars before the Impact.

And now it was a bounty on her son.

"Get Garcia and Danny. I want to check something out," the Raven said to one of his men.

Shayna pushed her way through the crowd, back toward the marquee. The hat blew off her head again; she let it go. All she could focus on was getting home, getting the boys, and getting out of town before the Ravens--or somebody else--found them.

The smooth slate of the sky had grown charcoal billows, and the first hints of thunder rolled far off in the distance. Screams from the market assaulted her ears as she realized she was almost jogging down the road. She slowed her pace, not wanting to look suspicious.

"Wait!"

She felt for the gun in the bag, switched the safety off, pulled it out, and turned around. The gray-haired stand owner was chasing after her. He was unbuttoning the last button on his black shirt; it caught the air and flapped behind him like a cape.

"Don't come any closer. I don't know what you want with me, but you should leave me alone."

The man slowed his pace and put his hands up, but kept walking forward. His shirt and hair flapped in the wind. "My name is Gabriel, and I know who you are," he said. "I want to help you."

"Not another step!"

The man stopped. "I know you're Cain's mom. He's one of us." He motioned to his white shirt with the flag on it. "I need you to get to him and relay a message."

"I don't have time for this. Did you hear what that guy just said! Every person in five counties will be looking for him!"

"I know that. But we knew that might happen someday. I also know that your oldest son, I'm sorry, I don't know what his real name is. Cain calls him Big--"

"Big Dummy, he calls him Big Dummy," she said with a heavy sigh. Her heart ached for Frank. She hated that so many people only knew him by Cain's hateful nickname. "But his name's Frank. And what'd you mean we knew this might happen? I don't know you."

"I know that Frank's seventeen and unregistered with the Ravens. Cain works with us, patriots--the resistance. We're trying to weaken the Ravens and do our part to help the U.S. government establish control again. I thought you'd recognize the shirt when I showed you in the market and would know I'm safe."

She shook her head. "There's no U.S. government anymore. And if there is, somewhere, I'm sure the military has enough weapons to wipe out the Ravens without much problem."

"Lord knows it's not quite that simple. People will protect the Ravens and fight for them because the Ravens have their sons. And they know they'll kill them. We're working to weaken that hold on the community by helping boys escape before they register. Trying to deplete assets if we can. We--"

"You're taking boys and leaving the families? Don't you think the Ravens will come back on the families for justice? You saw what just happened up there. They killed everybody. You're signing death sentences. I want no part of it."

Gabriel ran his fingers through his long gray hair. "Cain believes in our mission. He's been working for us for the better part of a year. Our team was losing faith. I asked God to guide me, and if our mission was His will, to help me understand how to move forward. He sent us your son."

"Well, thanks to your *sign from God* my son is probably going to die!"

He put his hand on her shoulders and bent to her eye level. She started to pull away but held her ground. This close, his fierce eyes seemed to soften a bit; they took on a much more tired and wise look.

"No, he won't. God has a plan for him. I'll see to it your family is safe, but you have to listen to me and do exactly as I say. First, you have to get your sons out of that house. The Ravens might not know where you live yet, but that bounty is high enough, someone will find you and tell them."

He looked back over his shoulder and bowed his head. She followed his gaze. The first body, probably Paul, was already hanging from the marquee. No kicking or fighting left, just the motionless silhouette of a man against the darkening sky.

Lake Brenton: Happiest Place in the Midwest.

"Tell Cain to get you and Frank to the abandoned church. He'll know where that is. I'll have men there to get y'all to safety until this blows over."

She nodded and turned to leave.

"One more thing I always tell our guys, I'll tell you too. If you get confronted by Ravens, remember they thrive on fear. Don't let them see that you're afraid. They're bullies. If you aren't afraid, they lose half their power. Don't do anything stupid, but don't let sense the fear. Got it?"

"Bullies with guns, who don't think twice about doing"--she pointed at the marquee--"that to people, usually make me afraid."

"But if they've already got ya, you got nothing to lose by not backing down."

She nodded again and hurried down the street. As she crested the hill, she took one last look back. Gabriel knelt, his head turned skyward. She didn't know why she trusted him, but she did. Something in the way his eyes looked up close. Grandfatherly almost. She hoped she wasn't making a mistake.

When she got back to the house that she'd left Gordon at, she pulled the truck around back and honked the horn three times. She held her breath. Gordon didn't appear in the back door. A few seconds that felt like minutes ticked by. She honked again. Nothing.

She grabbed the gun and sprinted for the house, leaving the truck running. Her gut clenched as she passed the pink rain slicker.

"Gordon?"

She rounded the corner into the living room. The couch was overturned like it was earlier. She dropped to her knees and peered under the couch. The long hair from the wig flopped in her face; she jerked it off and tossed it across the room.

Empty.

"Gordon! Where are you!"

Ideas raced through her head. Had he gotten scared that she'd turn him in and bolted? Had the Ravens tracked him here? She imagined Gordon stuttering pleas for help as they tossed the rope over his neck and winched him off the ground, the big Raven with his milky eyes watching and smirking. "Shouldn't have tried to escape, Gordon, you big dummy," he said as Gordon's body went limp. She forced the image out of her head.

But that name again. The thought made her shiver.

Tears overpowered her. They intensified every time she tried to take a breath and calm herself. She stared at the gun, its dark barrel blurred into blackness through her tear-riddled vision. Death was all around her. In the pink rain slicker, the bodies hanging above the marquee, Allen, probably all her friends from before Impact, and now her boys had been all but sentenced to death. Gordon and those eyes more than likely not far behind. Her world was little more than scorched earth and dead bodies. Maybe the world would be better off without her. The gun felt light in her hand. She put it in her mouth; her finger touched the trigger. She closed her eyes.

The tears hit her even harder.

Pulling the gun out of her mouth, she turned it toward the wall and pulled the trigger.

Click.

She pulled the trigger again.

Click.

She released the magazine into her hand. Empty.

Gabriel's voice floated into her memory. "Now, ya need to go get your sons and get out of that house."

Shame wrapped around her like a straightjacket. She didn't fight it. What she thought about doing was cowardly. She almost left her babies to the Ravens. Almost left her babies to suffer and be killed at the hands of that milky-eyed bastard.

She dropped the gun, pushed herself off the floor, and sprinted for the truck. When she opened the truck door, she heard the first rumbles of thunder. Only she knew it wasn't thunder.

It was motorcycles.

And she was only a few minutes ahead of them.

Chapter 3

Cain tossed himself onto his side and folded the pillow over his ear. Frank was snoring again, and no matter how hard he tried to tune it out it felt louder by the minute. Counting cracks in the ceiling didn't help. Trying to imagine what it would have felt like to win a state cross country championship didn't help either. Every inhaled breath echoed in his head. He sighed and kicked at Frank's mattress. Frank made a couple of indiscernible sounds and quieted for a minute or two but soon resumed snoring. Cain flopped to his back and completely covered his head with his pillow. No better. He threw it at his brother, but the snores didn't even change rhythm.

"Screw my life," he said.

The sound of truck tires on the gravel road outside provided something else to try to distract him from the rumbling. He thought it had to be his mom; no one else would be out here. That gravel road went two miles from the highway to their house, and the only other houses that used it were long since deserted and scavenged for anything that could be bartered. It had to be her truck coming down the gravel, but normally on market days, she didn't get home until around lunchtime. A look at his watch confirmed she was earlier than normal, and it sounded like she was moving fast.

That wasn't like his mother. She was normally overly cautious. Always complaining that he didn't wear a disguise when he went into town. Complaining that he drove too fast. Complaining that if he didn't negotiate better, they'd run out of seeds and not be able to get the things they needed. There wasn't much about him that she didn't complain about.

The engine raced as the truck rounded the bend, then the sound of gravel spraying as she buried the brake pedal and brought the truck to a stop in front of the house. Rocks dinged off some cars parked out front that he used for parts. He never heard the truck door slam but heard her footfalls coming up the wooden steps to the front porch. It sounded like she was running.

"The hell?" he muttered as he sat up on his mattress and pulled the blanket up to cover his scrawny chest. His shoulder-length black hair hung limp and straight to the sides of his smallish face, framing his deep green eyes. His face was deeply tanned and smooth. He'd missed out on the acne that most boys his age got, and he hadn't had to shave yet. Looking at his flawless skin, a person could easily have mistaken him for twelve instead of fifteen.

"If she comes in here and starts in again, I'm out," he thought. *"I'm done. I don't need her... or him. I'm better off on my own."*

Another long rumble from his brother's bed disrupted his thought.

The door flung open and smashed into the wall behind it. Cain scowled.

"Cain! They're coming! The Ravens are looking for you and Frank. Get--"

"Wh-what?" he said, barely able to disguise the disdain on his face. "What are you talking about?"

"They know, the Ravens. They know you've been helping hide kids. Like Gordon. He's alive. He escaped. Long story. I'll explain later, but you gotta get hidden and keep Frank quiet while I get rid of them. Gabriel says you should take us all to the abandoned church. Said you'd know what he meant." She hurried to the window.

"Shit."

Cain sat there and was unable to speak for a moment while everything she said whirred through his still foggy head.

"Frank!" Shayna dropped to her knees and shook her eldest son, shooing away his cat. It stood, hissed at her, then lay back down on Frank's feet. "Frank, wake up!"

Frank blinked his eyes and smiled.

"Hi Momma," he said and reached out his arms to hug her.

"Frank, there's no time. Cain, get your brother into the closet and keep him quiet until I tell you to come out!"

Scowling, Cain pushed and kicked the blankets onto the floor. He stomped to the window and looked out. He couldn't yet see the tell-tale dust cloud raised by tires on gravel, but he could hear the engines. Sounded like three of them, all motorcycles.

"Seriously, you're always saying I need to negotiate better. I'll just make 'em a deal. I'll turn him over, and I'll walk free?" Cain said. He glanced at his hulkish brother who was busy sliding on his jeans and a t-shirt. "They'll decide he's more trouble than he's worth and put him out of my misery.

Smack!

Cain's head jerked to the side; his cheek felt like a hundred needles poked him all at once. Warmth rushed to his face and seeped down to the back of his neck. The red hand mark quickly disappeared as the rest of his dark face blossomed to match it.

He turned his head back to face his mom; her eyes, once almost a sapphire blue like Frank's, were now being slowly muted by a milky haze, damage from exposure to the fog and rain. It had been a while since he'd looked at her this closely, and he was a little taken aback by how frail she appeared. The "acid eyes" aged her. But it wasn't just that, there was a deeper melancholy about her. His anger ebbed a bit, but a quick glance at his brother and he steeled himself against the fleeting moment of empathy.

"Well I guess that's one move you should know pretty well, shouldn't you," he said. Unable to stare at her wounded, haunted eyes, he looked toward Frank, who was dressed and sitting in the closet. "Is the big dummy over there gonna kill you now too?"

"Your brother didn't mean for that to happen, and you know it"--tears balanced on the bottom of her eyes--"it was an accident. He thought he was defending me." One of the tears broke over the wall and rolled down her cheek. She inhaled and breathed out as if trying not to let it become a deluge.

Cain turned back toward the window. Hearing her make excuses for Frank ignited a fire in his gut. The look on his dad's face, blood exploding from his shattered nose, his eyes rolling back in his head, the dull thud when his head hit the wall behind him, Frank roaring, his mother screaming and running to hug Frank. It all ran through his mind in vivid high-definition.

His dad stood over his mom. He'd thrown her against the wall and choked her. One of her kicks collided with his inner thigh. It missed its target but was close enough for him to let her go. He stepped back a couple of feet to get enough distance for another right cross. Frank cried for him to stop. Cain yelled for Frank to shut up and stay out of it before they both got it too. Alan stared at Frank and said "You should listen to your brother, big boy. Walk away before you get some of this too." Then he laughed at Frank. "Sissy boy. You better walk away. Listen to your brother." He swung and landed the right upside their mom's jaw. The impact lifted her up. She curled into the fetal position and cried for him to stop. Frank roared. Really roared. One punch was all it was. One crazed, rage-fueled punch. Mid-laugh, Allen's nose crunched. Blood exploded across the room. Allen's eyes rolled back. His head struck the wall behind him hard enough to leave a dent. He slid down, landing face first on the floor at Cain's feet. Shayna cried and rushed to Frank. His dad was dead at his feet, and his mom was worried about Frank!

Cain clenched his fist and banged it down on the window sill. He tried to think about something else but wasn't any more successful than he had been at blocking out Frank's snoring.

His mother's hand on his back jerked him out of his thoughts. He jerked away eyeing the dust rising through the thin trees that covered the hills. Tires crunched on the loose gravel.

"They're close," he said.

"Shit! I gotta get outside. Keep your brother quiet!" She hurried out of the room, shutting the door behind her. A few seconds later she appeared in the yard, reached into the truck, and slung her bag over her neck.

Cain glanced at his brother, shook his head, and pushed the closet door shut. "Don't make a peep, Dummy," he said.

"Cain! Don't leave me in here by myself," Frank said in a loud whisper. "Cain!"

Cain sighed and opened the door a crack, peeking in. Frank was trembling. He had wedged himself in the corner, his knees pulled up to his chest. His blue eyes, wild with fear, peered over his knees. Frank was only two years older, but had the appearance of a full-grown man; he was tall, muscular, and had a full black beard. He stood six-foot-three but seemed much younger and smaller cowering in the back of the closet like a scared puppy in a cage.

He looks like Gordon. Well, what Gordon looked like when they hauled him away.

Cain's gut suddenly burned. He felt the shame like a garrote, choking the air from him. He couldn't look at Frank's blue eyes anymore and turned around.

But she said he's alive... and he escaped.

He almost wished Gordon hadn't escaped. The thought of the disappointment that was surely lurking in Gordon's eyes curdled his stomach. Choking shame wrapped its warm hands around him again; he sucked in a long breath of air trying to fight it off. He could have done more that day. He should have done more that day. Gordon depended on him for protection, and he failed.

His grip on the doorknob loosened, allowing the white in his knuckles to fade back to a normal color. He opened the door about half-way.

"Okay, I'll leave this open if you promise me you'll be quiet. Deal?"

Frank nodded.

"And if I shut the door, it's because I have to, and that means you absolutely gotta be quiet. You know what the Ravens'll do if they catch you? They'll make you a slave. They'll beat you with a whip. If you get confused, or scared, or cry like you do sometimes, they'll whip you some more. And they'll kill Momma for not turning you over to them when you turned seventeen like she was supposed to."

Frank rocked back and forth. Tears flowed freely down his cheeks.

Cain's gut burned again.

"I don't wanna go with the Ravens, Cain," he repeated several times, each one quieter. Finally, he stopped rocking and stared straight ahead. "Will they really kill--"

His words were drowned out by the barrage of motorcycle engines racing around the last corner of the little country road to the house. Cain pursed his lips and held his finger in front of them. Frank nodded and pulled his knees back to his chest.

Cain crawled to the window and peered over the edge. The leaden sky pressed down on the hills beyond the house. The hills that once looked like they were draped with emerald green blankets were now a mix of mottled greenish-yellow and gray. The muted light that managed to penetrate the heavy clouds mingled with the fog to cast a sickly murk over everything.

His mom leaned on the hood of one of the abandoned cars that he had brought home. Her arms crossed in front of her chest. She pulled the twine out of her hair, letting it fall around her shoulders. A plastic bag blown by the wind attached itself to the car's antenna, flapped there a few seconds, then freed itself and blew down the driveway until it was tossed back into the air by the passing bikes. She stood straight as three motorcycles slid to a stop in front of her.

The man in the center got off his bike and appraised the area. He was about six-foot-five and built solid, but not overweight. He wore short sleeve collared shirt tight enough that his shoulders rippled as he removed his sunglasses, revealing a severe case of acid eyes. His beard was trimmed short, and his brown hair was combed to one side and showed the slightest hint of gray on his temples. On one side of his belt, he carried a bullwhip, the other a wooden baton. Other than the weapons, he could have passed for a college professor rather than a merciless killer.

Cain strained to see if he was concealing a gun, but couldn't spot one. With a case of acid eyes as bad as he had, he would have to get lucky to hit anything he aimed at anyway. His henchmen were the muscle. He took a quick inventory of them too. They looked very different. The both sported long blonde hair, one tied it back in a ponytail, and the other let it hang in loose and wavy. They both wore leather pants and leather vests with a screeching Raven embroidered on the back. They looked fairly young, mid-twenties maybe as opposed to the bigger man who looked about forty. But neither one was openly displaying a gun.

Subtlety wasn't something the Ravens were known for. They normally didn't mess around. They wanted you to be scared. When they snatched Gordon, they had four guys and a Capo. Two of the henchmen carried assault rifles, and the Capo carried a sawed-off shotgun. The idea that they'd come all the way out to the homestead with only three men and no guns was almost unconscionable.

Cain's gut burned again, this time from lack of respect.

Why would they respect you? When you had a chance to kill a couple of them, you hid like a scared kid and watched them haul Gordon away. You ain't hard. You're just a scrawny kid. Hell, even your so-called friends call you Skinny Cain. That ain't a compliment, kid.

Cain squinted his eyes and tried to force the voice out of his head.

"Nice place you got here," the man said, sliding on a pair of eyeglasses that enhanced his professorial look. He stepped forward and extended his hand. "I'm Poe. Your husband around?"

The boys' mother glanced at the Raven's hand but didn't offer hers in return.

"Poe? Did your parents name you that, or is it some sort of post-Impact rebirth kinda BS?"

Poe pulled his hand back and placed it on the stock of a bullwhip hanging from his belt. He chuckled; his bulk moved with his laughter but didn't shake. His bulk was power, not puff.

"Poe as in Edgar Allen. The man who created The Raven."

"Y'all didn't impress me as the book-readin' types," she said in a faux southerly drawl that Cain had never heard before. She leaned against the junked car and tilted her head to one side.

"Cain! Cain! What's goin' on?" Frank said from the closet.

Cain bent low under the window sill. "Shhhh! Nothing," he said, then peered back over the sill.

Poe smiled and looked at the ground. "Boys, looks like we got ourselves a little spitfire," he said, looking over his shoulders at the other two. "Well actually, Miss, before the world fell apart, I taught American Literature at Hillsboro University." He unsnapped the button holding the whip in place with a dexterous flick of his fingers. Free from its bonds, the whip spread into wider rings. Its cracker slipped free and dangled next to Poe's calf. "Danny, I think this pretty lady disrespected us and said we were too stupid to read books."

The blond with the long flowing hair grinned and nodded, but didn't speak.

"Maybe she needs something in her mouth to shut her up," the ponytailed blond said.

"Yeah, maybe she does, Garcia," Poe said, without turning toward the other man. "Again, Miss, I'd like to speak with your husband."

"Husband died a year ago. It's just me."

"I'm sorry to hear about your husband. Truly. I guess you and I have a little business we need to take"--he reached up and slid one finger along the side of her face, then grabbed her by the chin and held her--"care of. How's a pretty lady like you survive out here all by yourself without registering any kind of growing operation?"

She tried to pull herself free, but Poe tightened his grip. Cain was thankful that Frank couldn't see it. He didn't have the mental skills to make decisions based on weighing possible outcomes. And he didn't understand his strength. The last time he'd seen someone touch his momma, he lost control and killed his father with one punch. Cain understood there was a difference between a drunk, skinny, wife beater and three armed, well-trained fighters; Frank didn't.

"Get your hands off me, you pig," she said as best she could with how tightly he gripped her cheeks.

Shayna reached into the pocket of her overalls and pulled out a plastic bag of seeds. She pushed it into Poe's chest.

"Here! Here's your share of my hard work."

Poe released her, but loud red marks from his thumb and forefinger highlighted her face. He held up the bag of seeds and turned it around, then tossed it to Garcia. "What we got there?" he asked.

Garcia opened the bag and fingered his way through it.

"Pretty nice, boss. About a half pound, maybe a little more. Good selection of stuff. She's doin' pretty well out here, I'd say."

Poe smiled, his teeth were yellower than the oppressive air. "That's a decent little contribution, Miss," he paused. "I don't think I got your name."

"Prospero. Miss Prospero," Shayna said, making eye contact and holding it.

Poe laughed again.

"Very clever, Miss... Prospero. What a brilliant choice of names, Masque of the Red Death, right? But, you sure you want to stick with that name? I think your name is Coldrake. But, we can play your game and stick with Prospero. You

know how the story ends, right? Prospero dies...
and then so do all the people he was hiding."

The color ran from Shayna's face.

"Yes, I was just getting around to the real
reason for this little visit. I'm looking for a
seditionist. Seems you've been hiding quite a lot.
Prospero's a very accurate name indeed. You
know anybody named Skinny Cain?"

Cain ducked under the sill again.

"Shit!" he whispered. His heart beat so hard it
threated to shake his whole body. They weren't
here about unpaid tithes; they were looking for
him. He knew he had to get Frank and try to make
a run for it. There was a crawlspace under the
greenhouse that should work to hide them for a
while. He had a gun in the truck out back--if he
could get to it--that'd give them an advantage.
Even if the Ravens found the crawlspace, he'd be
able to get off four or five shots as soon as they
opened the door and hopefully take a couple out.

But they had to get there.

He crawled to the closet and opened the door.
Frank--still with his knees pulled to his chest--
rocked back and forth and trembled.

He heard Poe outside: "Danny, you and
Garcia go and check the house. Little spitfire
Prospero here, was way too willing to part with a
lot of seeds. She's hiding something. Probably the
son."

"Come on!" Cain said, standing up. At this
point, he figured it didn't matter if they saw or

heard him. They were coming regardless. "We gotta get out of here!"

Frank didn't move. His big eyes oozed sadness... and fear.

Cain cringed.

Gordon. This is gonna end just like Gordon.

He put his hand on Frank's arm, bent down, and looked directly into those blue eyes without turning away. "Frank! We gotta go! The Ravens are coming!"

Chapter 4

The Ravens climbed off their bikes and started toward the house. Shayna knew she had to try to buy Cain a little time to get out of the house and into the woods behind the greenhouse. She opened the truck door into Danny and sprinted for the front porch. She got to it first and blocked the steps, her arms outstretched and holding the handrail on either side. Garcia grabbed her by both shoulders and pulled her face close to him; she strained against it, but he was too strong.

"Yeah, those lips are to die for. Uhhhh! I got somethin' you're gonna enjoy, and if you don't well, I'm still gonna enjoy it." He made a kiss-face at her. "You are somethin' special."

"You might not like it as much as you think. I'm a spitter." She leaned back and spat in his face. It struck him just above his right eye and dripped down his cheek like a giant teardrop.

He released her and retreated a step. But before she could gather herself he wiped at his eye, then swung his fist, landing a punch square in her stomach. She released her grip on the rails. Her hands flew to her gut. She gasped for air and plopped down on the step behind her. Garcia grabbed the back of her overalls and flung her into the yard. She rolled over three times, finally coming to rest face-down in the dirt.

"I'll be back for those lips, that's a promise," Garcia said.

She pushed herself to her hands and knees. Still gasping, her elbows threatened to yield under the pressure.

"Run!" she croaked.

Her elbows failed. She sucked in a mouth full of dirt. Thunder rumbled off to the south. She lay her head on the dirt. The dirt that used to be grass. Bright green grass that was full of life, like she used to be. Before her life changed. She cursed herself for her self-pity. Frank and Cain's lives changed too. She ran down a list of things that most teenagers enjoyed that they'd never experience: Prom night, sneaking booze into the football games, and unless they got away from the Ravens, their next birthdays.

The embarrassment gave her strength. It surged through her arms. She pushed herself back up.

Someone grasped her overalls from behind and jerked her to her feet.

Garcia winked and nodded toward Shayna. He dropped a backpack on the porch and kicked the wooden door. It shook but held. The 'Welcome Friends' sign that she'd brought out here from the city crashed to the deck. He kicked the door again, and it exploded inward.

Shayna saw Cain and Frank coming out of the bedroom, and all three made brief eye contact. Cain reached back for Frank's hand.

"Run, Frank! Run--"

The cold steel of a knife blade pressed against her throat.

"You better shut the hell up, before I shut you up," a voice growled in her ear.

Chapter 5

Cain pulled on Frank's hand and bolted toward the back door. It was too late for the greenhouse idea. The Silverado pickup that he'd found last week was just outside the back door. If they could get to it, he could plow through the bikes and escape. Their mom could hop in the back as they drove past. Or not, he honestly didn't care all that much, but Frank would be inconsolable if they left her behind.

Frank bumped the corner as Cain pulled him around the door frame. It wasn't much of a delay, but it was enough. Garcia jumped on Frank's back. Frank rumbled forward like an out-of-control semi-truck only regaining balance once he crashed into the faux-oak paneled living room wall. Frank's shoulder broke through. Garcia groaned but held tight. Frank bounced back and kept his legs moving.

He tried to tug Garcia's arm free from his neck as he moved. They crashed side to side as they headed down the hall. Frank spun and bashed Garcia against the wall; his grip loosened momentarily, but he still clung on. The extra weight slowed him, but he was still only a couple steps behind Cain reaching the back door.

Garcia tried to wedge his legs between Frank's moving ones. Finally, he got a leg jammed in there. Frank took a stride but met the resistance of Garcia's lower leg. Frank pushed as hard as he could. Garcia's tibia snapped; he screamed in agony. He rolled off Frank's back and landed hard on the ground. He rolled over and reached for Frank's foot but missed. He screamed again.

Cain reached the truck and jumped behind the wheel. He felt under the dash for the wires he needed and turned over the engine. Revving it, Cain reached back under the seat, found the Beretta .45, and laid it on the seat. He didn't know if Frank had it in him to shoot someone, but hopefully just firing off rounds would make the Ravens take cover long enough to give them a bit of an opening.

Frank swung the door open and fell into the cab. Cain stomped on the accelerator. The truck spun up dirt and fishtailed before gaining traction and lurching forward. Garcia had pulled himself up on the porch railing, agony still carved on his young looking face. Cain noted that Danny hadn't followed them out the door, as the truck rounded the corner of the house he saw why. Danny stood in the center of the driveway, one hand using their mother's hair to pull her neck back, the other holding a long-bladed knife to her exposed throat.

"Momma!" Frank cried.

Cain slammed on the brakes, jolting them both forward.

"Take it easy, Frank. Stay calm. You hear me? Just follow me and stay close."

Cain slipped the gun into the back waistband of his jeans. "Let me talk, and follow my lead" he whispered to Frank.

He opened the truck door and stepped out, holding both hands in the air. He heard Frank's door clang shut too, but he didn't back look to see if he was following as instructed. Hopefully, he was, but beyond that, he hoped his brother wouldn't overreact to someone threatening his precious momma. He needed Frank to trust him and not go rogue and get them both killed. Unfortunately, he hadn't given Frank much reason to trust, or even like, him over the last year or so. He shut his eyes and gave a quick, silent prayer that Frank had a short memory.

Cain eased his way toward the group, his hands in the air. Up close, Danny appeared much older than Garcia. His cheeks were losing their elasticity, and his skin had the weathered look of many summers in the sun. Cain thought he must have worked outdoors Pre-Impact, maybe a farmer or lawn care or something. His wavy blond hair had thick streaks of gray mixed in. Deep lines ran from the corners of his eyes. The hand holding the knife shook a bit.

Cain looked Danny in the eye. They fluttered wide open and the whites spread out, threatening to overtake the brown. Gravel rattled as he dug in with his feet. He didn't look comfortable holding a woman's life in his hands. He didn't look like he even really wanted to be a soldier. The ones that weren't true believers could sometimes be reasoned with. He flipped a Raven soldier about six months ago. The kid went full double-agent and spilled some decent intel that kept Gabriel busy for weeks trying to verify. But that kid was young and had nothing to lose. This guy was older, probably wiser; the Ravens were likely leveraging him with something precious. Wife? Kids? Cain didn't know, but the guy seemed like he'd rather be a hundred other places, and that was good. The fact that he was holding a blade and not a gun was better.

"I'm surrendering," he said. "Why don't you let her go?" He nodded toward his mother, who wasn't struggling against Danny's grip but wasn't acquiescing either. She stood firm and focused on her youngest son. He avoided her gaze, instead stealing a quick glance at his older brother next to him. Frank's chest heaved, and his raised hands shook. "I'm the one you're looking for, right? Skinny Cain, right?"

"Son, don't--"

Cain's eyes darted around the scene looking for any possible escape route in case trying to talk his way out went sideways. Without knowing for sure if any of the Ravens had a gun made the decision harder. If the Ravens knew they were looking for "Skinny Cain," they'd know he was part of the resistance movement and probably armed. The thought of them coming to get him without being armed to the teeth was almost unconscionable. He looked to see if they had snipers around the bend. Nothing... that he could spot. If Garcia had been armed, he would've had it out when he burst through the door. Poe's acid eyes would prevent him from being too accurate even if he was armed, and Danny had a knife and not a gun to his mom's throat. As far as he could tell, they really came all the way out there to apprehend him without a single gun.

The Ravens must have expected that intimidating a widow and a couple of teenagers was going to be easy. Must have thought this would be a quick run on a soft target. They were caught unprepared and under-armed. Cain knew that gave him an advantage. As much as it made his gut burn that they'd so blatantly underestimated him, he wanted to keep that advantage.

They really don't respect you, let alone fear you. You got lucky scaring a boy, these are men, and you're just the same scared kid that let them take Gordon.

"C'mon. You want me, not some old widow. She didn't have any idea what I was doing," he said. "Hell, she barely knows me." He tried to make his voice sound much more confident than he was feeling.

Cain saw the hurt flash across his mom's face. Guilt brushed its acid over him. A quick glance at his brother next to him, shaking with silent tears streaming down his face washed the guilt away. She wasn't really worried about him; she was worried about Frank. It was always Frank. And somehow, she'd come to expect him to be just as concerned about Frank as she was. Like hell! If she wanted that burden, good for her, but she wasn't going to push it off on him. Screw that!

But yet here he was with the responsibility to try to get them all out of here in one piece and with no idea how he was going to do it.

Of course, it falls on you. It's your fault the Ravens are even out here.

"Cain... no," Frank said.

Now Frank is defending you. You're pathetic. Gordon would probably make excuses for you too, even after you stayed hidden and let the Ravens haul him away. Can you be any less of a man?

"You're Skinny Cain? Yeah right," Danny said. "No way."

Cain's face flushed red, and the anger boiled inside him.

"I am Skinny Cain. You know your boy, Noah Meyer? He can identify me. 'Course he might not want to since I put a bullet in his shoulder. He had powder burns by the wound, didn't he? That's 'cause I could've killed him, but didn't. Two guys were holding him down. All I had to do was put the gun next to his head and end him. I didn't, though. I shot him point-blank in the shoulder. Made sure to get the joint so it would be good and screwed up for the rest of his life. Then he wouldn't be any good to you guys and could go free."

Some of the color drained from Danny's face. That was what Cain wanted to see. The story must've hit home. He obviously recognized the details. But the color quickly returned, and he readjusted his grip on Shayna and jerked her head back harder.

Encouraged, he continued, "C'mon, man. You know I'm telling you the truth now. Let the woman go, and I'll come with you. You and I both know you're just doing this because they've got someone you love held hostage. Just like you're doing right here," Cain said in a soft, calm voice.

He slowly lowered his hands to his side. He watched for any sign that he might have hit another nerve. If he had, Danny wasn't showing it.

"Take me and let the woman and the big dummy here go. Whatcha say?"

"You're a disgusting little puke," Danny said. His knife hand shook badly. His eyes bulged until they seemed to cover most of his face save his crooked yellow teeth. "You're all gonna hang!"

"Take just you? Not a chance," Poe said, stepping down from the front porch. "No. No. No. You hurt my man, and now I hurt yours, that's how the game is played. Did you hear the screams coming from my guy in there? You hurt him bad. Now it's my turn."

"Did you hear him say he was the one that shot Meyer?" Danny said.

Poe smiled. "Is that so? This little kid?" He spun the baton as he walked. It thumped the air like a fan blade. He covered the space between them and the porch in what seemed like two strides. Shayna struggled against Danny's grip, her eyes wide. Air from the spinning baton batted at the front of her hair. She twisted her shoulders trying to get leverage. Danny's knife hand shook more, nicking her with the blade. A crimson flower bloomed on the side of her neck.

Cain nodded. He didn't want to break eye contact with Danny but could see Frank's big body shaking next to him. "Easy, Frank," he whispered.

"Let Momma go!" Frank roared. His hands clenched into fists.

"What you gonna do there, big boy?" Poe said. "You want some of this?" Poe slapped the palm of his hand with the baton. He glared at Frank. Frank didn't budge. "Boy, you too dumb to know when you shouldn't challenge a man. I'd bash your skull with this thing, but you're too valuable. Big, strong boy like you'll bring a nice payday. Farms like big boys like you. And I like getting paid."

Without warning, Poe swung the baton. It whistled like a firework, culminating in the sickening crunch of bone breaking as it crashed into their mom's knee. It buckled. She dropped to the ground. Danny twisted her hair in his hand, trying to pull her back up. She rolled her back toward Poe. Danny tightened his grip. Another dark bloom appeared where the knife scraped her skin as she fell.

"Frank--" was all she got out. Her eyes told the rest of the story, pleading with her youngest son to stay calm.

Poe's face pulsed red. The baton thumped as he twirled it. He stepped closer to Frank and glowered at him. Turning his back to the brothers, he said, "But I want to play a new game. You hurt mine, I kill yours. That's how this new game works. Tell your momma goodbye, boy."

Poe swung the baton again, this time landing the blow across her kidneys. She screamed as her body bowed forward. Clumps of her hair pulled free; streams of blood from her scalp mixed with the tears on her face. She fell to her knees, pulling and writhing as much as she could against Danny's hold. He tugged on her hair, trying to drag her back to her feet. It only forced her bloody face upward toward Frank's eyes.

"Hold it right there, man, or I'll cut her. I'll kill her!" Danny said to Frank. The knife trembled and shaved away layers of skin. He used his other hand to grab her under the arm and pull her to her feet. His arm shook from straining to support her weight one-handed.

Cain looked around; he wasn't sure he could get to the gun and shoot both Poe and Danny before the other one could kill his mother. And he wasn't even sure he was a good enough shot to not hit her instead of Danny. Shooting targets or small game was one thing, shooting a human using his mother as a shield was something totally different. Panic clawed its way into his stomach.

Cain tried to make eye contact with his brother. Frank's normal pallid skin glowed like a painful sunburn; he was shaking as much as Danny. Trying to calm him would be useless, but he had to try.

"Frank, don't do anything stupid to get us all killed, you hear me?!"

"You should really listen to your brother," Poe said, laughing.

That did it. Frank snapped. Cain was sure he saw a quick flashback, race across his face.

Frank dove at Poe, striking him at the waist and knocking him backward. They fell to the ground, Frank's bulk coming to bear on Poe's ribcage. The crushing impact pushed the air from his lungs, stunning him. The baton fell from his hand and rattled across the driveway. Frank kicked and tried to dig his boot into the dirt for leverage, pushing the side of Poe's face into the gravel. Poe gurgled and gasped for air.

Cain reached for the gun tucked into his waistband, switched the safety off, aimed and fired twice. Too low. Two dark wet spots appeared on his mom's overalls. Her eyes bolted wide open, then faded, and her head slumped forward. Cain fired a third time, striking Danny in the head. The hazy yellow air briefly mixed with a red mist as he dropped backward. The knife slid across her throat as he fell. Her body collapsed forward, blood draining from her neck where Danny's knife had sliced it.

Frank had pushed himself free of Poe and was scrambling toward the baton when the shots rang out. He turned in time to see the third bullet strike Danny and the knife slide across his mother's throat.

"Momma!" he cried out, his rage choked out by tears. He forgot about the baton and lunged toward her slumping body. He scooped her up; she looked even more tiny and frail cradled in his enormous arms.

Cain tugged at his brother. "Frank! We gotta get out of here!"

Frank continued to rock his mom's limp body. Her shirt, completely soaked in blood, began to dampen his shirt as well. He mumbled to her between sobs.

Cain saw Garcia rummaging through the backpack, crutched by a long stick, his broken leg hung limp. He pulled out a radio and tossed the pack aside. Cain fired twice at him, but missed, splintering the wood door frame. Garcia ducked around the wall out of sight. Cain knew he was unarmed and couldn't escape. He started to run toward the door but decided they needed to get as far away as they could before the reinforcements arrived. Garcia would have to wait, other than with the radio, he wasn't a threat, and that damage was already done.

Frank still held his mom. He sobbed quietly and brushed her hair away from her blank eyes.

"Damnit, Frank! Run! Why are you so stupid! You gotta leave her. More Ravens are coming!"

Poe had pushed himself to all fours. Cain snatched the baton and brought it down across Poe's lower back. He bellowed in agony and fell flat again.

Cain hit him again, and a third time. Poe writhed on the ground. He lifted his head and screamed. Cain took a step forward and kicked him in the chin. Teeth shattered like frozen plastic. His head snapped back then thumped back onto the gravel. He didn't move.

When Cain turned his focus back to escaping, he saw that Frank had placed their mother's body in the truck bed and he was sitting with his back against the cab. His white tank top was red with blood, and he had blood smeared on his face. His knees were pulled up to his chest. He quivered with every new wave of sobs. Cain's frustration with his brother washed away.

"Frank, we can't take the truck. I'm just gonna move it up into the road. Then we're gonna run for it, okay?" Cain said, remembering Garcia and his radio. "They're too close, and it sounds like a lot of them. We gotta get into the timber. We can lose them there. Remember when mom and dad used to bring us out here when we were little, and we used to play in the ravine down by the creek? We'll head that way. If they try to follow us, we'll have a head start and know the area, okay?"

Frank nodded and slid his legs flat. "But what about Momma?"

"We gotta leave her, Frank. They will kill us if they catch us. We killed two of their men and hurt their boss." He reached his hand out to his older brother. "Let's go!"

Frank bent and kissed his momma's bloody forehead, smoothed her hair away from her eyes again, and scooted to the tailgate. He wiped tears away with his hands streaking the blood on his face into something like war paint. Cain handed him the baton and jogged toward the tree line. Frank followed, turning every few steps to look behind him.

Chapter 6

The timber didn't provide as much cover as Cain had hoped. The long winter following the Impact killed off many of the weaker trees, and the scorching heat and acid rain since slowly poisoned the ones that were left. The canopy, which once was almost impenetrable, now allowed streams of hazy light to illuminate the ground. Cain was thankful for the darkening skies to cast some gloom into the timber.

Since they were going to be easier to see than he'd hoped, he knew they had to try to get as much distance between them and the Ravens as they could. A half mile or so beyond the road, the woods spread out and surrounded the lake. The Ravens would have a much more difficult time following them with all that ground to cover.

The boys jogged along, dodging between the trees, a few thick and healthy, others dead and rotting but not yet toppled. Dry twigs snapped under their feet as they went. The sound of their progress was drowned out by a clap of thunder that rolled over the hills. It built to a deafening roar that shook the leaves around them.

Frank stopped and leaned against a tree trying to catch his breath.

"Stay here, I'm gonna run a little ahead and make sure we're where I think we are," he said. Frank nodded and sucked big gulps of air.

It had been several years since he'd run through these woods. When they were kids, they'd play out here all day while their parents worked on the homestead. He walked and looked around for a few minutes to get his bearings. It didn't take him as long as he thought it might to remember exactly where they were. The road was directly ahead. That was supposed to be as far as they were allowed to go when they were playing. One day, he told Frank that he was going to the other side. Frank didn't want to go, with him but Cain said he was going with or without him. Frank feared his little brother might get attacked by a wild animal so reluctantly agreed to go.

That summer, they snuck across the road every chance they could. They bonded over the thrill of their mutual defiance. They spent the summer days chasing each other all over the woods, playing Hide and Seek, Cops and Robbers, Cowboys and Indians, or any other game they could think up. Now they were running for their lives for real. Running from people who were much better trackers that his lumbering brother used to be.

Every time he thought about the gravity of their situation, his legs felt a little weak.

He hustled back to his brother who was still leaning against the tree. A few stray tears leaked out, rolling over their mother's bloody war paint. He was looking down at his hands. His fingers were intertwined; he was turning one thumb over

the other. It was something Momma had taught
him to do when he was scared, so he would quit
thinking about whatever was scaring him. His
momma was all he had; she knew how to comfort
him when he got upset, how to make him feel
strong. It was important that he had that security,
and Cain knew it. He just never cared much about
what his brother needed before. Frank had
Momma to worry about all his needs. Cain didn't
have anyone but himself to rely on and hadn't for
months. Frank's feelings and fears were the least
of his concerns.

Until a few minutes ago.

Until you filled his momma full of hot lead.

Cain tried to ignore the voice. He had to
concentrate on getting them both out of here alive.
If he could pull it off, he'd persuade the resistance
to smuggle Frank out of Raven controlled
territory.

*Yeah, right. You took his momma away, and
now you're just gonna ship him off into oblivion
all by himself. He'll die on his own. He'll suffer...
and then die! Like Gordon!*

"Okay, Frank, listen. The road is about a
quarter mile dead ahead. We're gonna cross it,
then we can head down the hill into the ravine.
Remember when we used to play over there?
There's that little creek. We'll follow it for a while
and then bust it up inside and head for the lake.
Got it? We need to hurry though. Get as far as we
can while they're stopped at the house before that
Garcia guy tells 'em where we went. I doubt they
have dogs out here, but just in case, take off your

shirt, it's covered in--" Cain saw Frank wrestle with sobs at the mention of the blood on his shirt. "It's dirty, leave it here. Maybe they'll think we stayed on this side of the road."

Frank nodded but looked like he was fighting the sobs that begged to wrack his body again. Cain could tell he was trying to act strong. He'd always acted like he was Cain's protector. Cain never let it bother him until he got old enough to realize that he'd spend his life taking care of his older brother. Since then, he resented every time Frank acted like he was the responsible one. Hated it even.

Frank peeled off the tank top and tossed it on a dead limb. It slid off, leaving a maroon stripe on the wood. Cain picked it up, ran a few feet and dropped it on another branch, leaving another mark. He repeated the process two more times, then left the shirt, wiped his hands on his pants, and hustled back to Frank.

"Hopefully they'll follow the blood marks and think we're headed that direction," he said.

They made their way toward the road, moving slowly to make less noise. They could hear bikes approaching. Cain listened. It sounded like at least six of them or maybe a few bikes and a truck. Maybe two. They weren't fooling around this time. They weren't going to underestimate a couple of teenage boys and a widow again.

But the widow's dead. They didn't kill her, you did. You might as well have just shot him too. He's all alone now!

A branch snapped in the timber behind them, distracting Cain from the voice in his head. The boys both dropped flat on the ground and peered through the trees. Surely, there couldn't be someone that close behind them already. They watched for a few minutes. More branches snapped, but no sign of anyone following.

Thunder rolled again, drowning out the engines momentarily. A breeze rattled the branches behind them. A few dried leaves tumbled across the ground and piled themselves next to a downed tree like an autumn colored snow drift. Cain couldn't see anyone, but as soon as the thunder died out, he heard something moving through the underbrush behind them.

"Holy crap! Have they really caught up with us that fast? We gotta move," Cain whispered. "Crawl to the tree line, then sprint across the road and don't stop until you're several feet inside the tree line on the other side. Then lie back down. I'll be right behind you."

The wind gusted, and thunder crashed around them again. Frank crawled to the edge of the trees. He moved into a squatting position. Another snap behind them caused him to freeze, turn, and look for Cain, his eyes wide and wild. Cain nodded him forward just as the thunder died out. The roar of the engines filled his ears.

They were closer than he thought they were!

"Frank!" he hissed, quickly looking behind to see if whoever was tracking them was within sight. No one. "Frank!" he tried to whisper as loud as he could but was afraid to yell.

It was too late. Frank sprinted out of the tree line and down into the roadside ditch. He lunged up the other side, but lost his footing on some loose rocks, sending him sliding down the embankment. He groaned and reached for his left ankle. He rubbed it for a few seconds then pushed off with his right leg and bounded up the side of the ditch and into the road. The bikes sounded like they were just around the curve and moving fast. Frank limped toward the center of the road, barely touching his left foot to the ground.

"Frank! Run!"

Snap! Snap!

Those were closer. Some dead leaves rustled followed by another couple snaps.

The vehicles started around the bend in the road only about three-hundred yards from being able to see Frank. Three bikes and two trucks. A dome of dust hung in the air behind them. The second truck lagged a bit. Two guys stood in its bed hanging onto the roll bar. They each had an assault rifle hung over their shoulder. He couldn't see well enough through the dust to tell what kind but knew it meant that the Ravens weren't fooling around.

Cain took another quick look behind him. Still nothing.

Frank slid down into the ditch on the other side, dragging his right hand through the loose dirt to keep his balance. He groaned loud enough for Cain to hear when his foot hit the bottom of the embankment.

"Please get down. Please get down," Cain mumbled. He pulled the .45 out again in case they saw movement and stopped. He knew there were at least five bullets left and he'd use them all if needed. Not that his five bullets would do much good, but hopefully he'd hit a couple of them, and the chaos would give Frank time to get further into the woods. He steadied the gun at the point where he thought they might stop.

Frank climbed up the other embankment and hobbled toward the tree line. With each step, he was using his left foot less and less. A heavy, dead branch on the ground tripped him. He screamed and dove for the tree line. The underbrush swallowed up his man-sized body.

The Ravens roared past, leaving the dome of dust hanging over the road.

Cain tucked the gun away and sprinted down the ditch. It felt like he was running out in the open for miles before disappearing into the cover of the dust cloud. He charged up the other side of the ditch and into the road. Between the dust and the natural camouflage, Frank wasn't visible inside the tree line, but its safety looked impossibly far away.

He lowered his head and ran as fast as he could. The loose gravel slipped under his feet, slowing him. He reached the edge of the road and leaped across the ditch. He landed barely short and banged his knee on a good-sized rock that poked out of the embankment. Pain shot up his leg and flashed like a strobe light across his vision. He ignored it and clawed at the rocks and dirt to pull his way to the top. He ran across the uneven ground toward the trees. Sticks on the ground rolled causing him to stumble like a drunken man.

He reached the cover of the tree line and collapsed on the ground next to Frank. He rolled to his back and struggled to catch his breath. He listened and heard the vehicles sliding in the loose rock as they rounded the final bend and saw the truck he left parked in their way.

The truck that you made him leave Momma in. Now they have her body. God only knows what they'll do to her.

"Crap," Cain said to himself.

Chapter 7

Garcia leaned forward as best he could and pressed both hands on Poe's chest. He'd tried to kneel, but the blinding white flash of pain from his mangled leg advised him otherwise. "One... two... three. One... two... three," he counted off as he worked on the chest compressions. Because of the way he had to lean, he wasn't able to get his full strength behind them. Each attempt felt more feeble and useless. Poe's bloody face stared silently at the sky without the tiniest rasp of breath. His jaw hung open at a funny angle, and there was a deep gash along his cheek where his glasses broke and sliced him like a ripe tomato.

Garcia did another set of compressions with no change. Panic gripped him. He knew he had to stay calm but couldn't remember ever being this scared. Or feeling this helpless. He had to maintain his composure. Failure was not an option. Neither was letting the others be able to figure out the truth because of his emotions. Poe would kick his ass if he let anyone find out their secret. That thought brought another wave of cold panic over him.

"C'mon! Breathe for Christ's sake! Don't leave me here!"

He did another set of compressions and leaned in closer to listen for any sound of life. He leaned too far, and his leg flashed its anger. He moved his hand to Poe's shoulder to steady himself and blinked his eyes trying not to pass out. He swallowed hard. Then he heard it. A gurgle deep in Poe's throat.

Adrenaline surged through him. It forced away the fear of passing out and deadened the pain in his leg a bit. Another set of compressions, another gurgle. Garcia willed himself onto one knee and put more of his weight behind the next set. The pain overpowered the adrenaline, but he ignored it and kept pushing. White edges of his vision pushed in on Poe's bloody face, blurring the gory details. Finally, he heard a breath. It was faint, but it was clear enough to give him hope; the sound of the bikes on the gravel gave him even more hope.

The reinforcements raced around the corner and barely missed the Silverado parked at the top of the drive. One guy laid his bike down on the loose rock. He tumbled across the ground; the motorcycle slid until it hit the front tires of the parked truck. It flipped up in the air and crashed down on the truck's hood.

Garcia jumped. "Jesus H. Christ!" he said.

The truck that was following the bikes swerved to miss the guy laying in the road. Gravel pelted Garcia. A rock hit his leg, sending a spike of pain rushing through him. He grimaced and clenched his teeth. The passenger door opened, and a man jumped out and ran to check on the guy who'd wrecked his bike. The driver ran toward Garcia and Poe. "Is he alive?" he said.

"Yeah. Barely," Garcia said through clenched teeth. His body throbbed from his toes all the way up to his chest cavity, a steady, painful drumbeat. "Doc didn't come with you?"

Garcia was relieved to see Dylan. He'd come on board two years ago, and he and Garcia had become fast friends. They were the same age, had the same athletic build, and even similar hair color. Many people said they could be brothers separated at birth. Garcia agreed; Dylan was the brother he never got to have.

Dylan shook his head. "Poe had him leading a raid on a house on the other side of town. Hung the parents in the market for hiding a probie. Sent Doc and a couple other guys"--he pulled up short and covered his mouth at the sight of Poe--"Whoa. A kid and an old lady did this?"

Poe's eyes bulged, one of them little more than a brown island in a sea of milky-red. His head arched back, and he took in a raspy breath.

"Probies! Get your asses over here," Dylan yelled.

Garcia shifted into a seated position and winced as another bolt of pain rattled him. "Christ, they sent probies out here? Did they even listen to me?" He patted Poe's motionless hand. "Hang in there, Boss. Here, Dylan, help me up.."

Dylan bent and flung Garcia's arm over his shoulder. "Ready?"

Garcia nodded. Dylan slowly raised up. Garcia inhaled through his gritted teeth and blew it out.

"You screwed that thing up good, huh?" Dylan said.

Garcia didn't reply. He kept inhaling and blowing until he was on one foot and only using Dylan for balance. Four fresh-faced recruits jogged over and stopped a few feet away. One of them was the guy who wrecked the bike; blood soaked through one side of his shredded jeans. A couple of them carried AR-15s, and they weren't even carrying them correctly. The fourth guy slipped the magazine out of his Glock and jammed a new one in. He was a little bulkier than the other three but looked younger. He had shaggy black hair and his feeble attempt at growing a beard made him look even less imposing. Their mouths gaped when they got a good look at Poe lying on the ground gasping for breath through his damaged teeth.

"Don't just stand there and stare, Probie. Get the truck backed over here, and get him in it! Now!"

The recruits scrambled to follow Dylan's orders. Garcia shook his head; he still couldn't believe they'd send him a bunch of probies. At least they were well armed. Now whether any of them knew how to handle those weapons, or had the nerve to actually kill another person, was still up for debate. Based on the looks on their faces when they saw Poe, he doubted it.

"I want those kids' heads. I mean it," Garcia said. He glanced down at Poe again and then hit the bed of the truck to signal the driver to stop. "If they can get them alive, better. But if they have to kill them, I want their goddamned heads literally ripped from their bodies and brought to me."

Three of them were working to lift Poe into the truck. The boy with the Glock had been giving directions, but paused and stared at Garcia. His face didn't show fear; it was more of a look of disdain. Garcia noticed.

"Got a problem?"

The kid didn't answer. He turned away and climbed up to help slide Poe into the bed of the truck.

"Who's that?" Garcia asked Dylan.

"Jovi Fields. His older sister's pretty hot. Golden Fields or something weird like that. His dad was the principal at Lake High before Impact. Wormy little guy. Not sure about mom. Kid's been okay so far. Not great, not terrible. Think he probably just wants to do his four years and get out."

"Get him down here."

Dylan shot Garcia a questioning look. Garcia didn't acknowledge it or even blink. He stared at Jovi, his jaw set. The throb in his leg fueled his anger. Another quick look at Poe made his pulse race. That heartbeat of pain pounded away, each beat more agonizing than the last, ratcheting up his rage.

Dylan motioned for Jovi to come. He nodded and hopped down out of the truck bed.

"You got a problem with me, Probie?" Garcia said, his pain punctuating each word.

Jovi looked at Garcia but didn't answer. His lower lip trembled.

Garcia pushed the kid into the truck's fender. He stepped forward, putting pressure on his broken leg. Pain jolted him. His eyes popped, and he felt like a hand was tugging on his heart. He quickly eased up on the bad leg and hopped forward on the other, grabbing Jovi by the shirt. He pulled the boy forward and shoved him back into the truck hard enough that the kid groaned.

"I asked if you had a problem with me."

Jovi shook his head.

"You gave me a look earlier. Did you see what those kids did to Poe? See my leg? They hurt one of ours, we kill one of theirs, right?"

"Yeah."

"You got the balls to kill someone, Probie. You look pretty goddamned weak to me. What if I gave you a choice: cut those brothers' heads off, or I'll personally kill your hot-piece-of-ass sister while you and your parents watch. Your dad used to be the principal at the high school, right? Could you do it? Or are you too freakin' weak?"

Poe sucked in a long breath that sounded like someone blowing bubbles in syrup. One of the probies shrugged off his denim jacket, rolled it up, and put it under Poe's head. "He's gotta get to a doctor. He's choking on his own blood over here."

Garcia paused for a second. "Dylan, you take this weak ass probie and head that way," he said, pointing in the direction Cain and Frank had fled. He jerked Jovi by the shirt and flung him into Dylan. He pointed at another of the recruits. "Take the AR that probie's got. He's gonna drive Poe and me to Doc so he won't need it. Can you get us there in one piece or do you drive like that putz?" He motioned toward the kid with the bloody jeans.

"Yes, sir. I can drive."

"You two,"--he pointed at the bloody jeans kid and the other one that carried an AR-15--"you go that direction. I want those two brothers. One's really big, the other one is small, but he's got a gun and killed Danny with it."

"Hey, Dylan! There's a dead woman in this truck" one of the other bikers that had been securing the perimeter yelled.

"That's the mom," Garcia said. "Get that body and put in the other truck and bring it back in."

Dylan acknowledged. He helped Garcia into the back of the truck next to Poe.

"Give me a gun," Garcia said. "Who knows if they've got more weapons hidden out there somewhere, and if they do, and they ambush us, I'm gonna get my shots in."

Dylan handed him a pistol. "See ya back at Nevermore," he said and banged twice on the side of the truck. The driver revved the engine and jammed the gas pedal down. The tires spun on the gravel. The truck fishtailed then surged forward.

Chapter 8

Cain sat up and flopped the curtain of black hair back out of his eyes with his fingers. He was still panting but was at least able to talk now. "How's your ankle?" he said.

"It hurts, Cain," Frank said. He moved his leg and winced.

"I need to take a look at it. It might hurt, but we gotta know how bad it is. Okay?"

Frank slid his jeans leg up a little bit, so his ankle was visible. It was sunset blend of red, yellow, and purple.

"Yeah, it's ugly. You sprained it pretty bad. Can you hobble on it until we can get to the creek? Then we can try to splint it. We just gotta get out of here... fast."

Cain nodded to Frank and pulled him up. He used a tree to help steady himself before trying to take a tentative step forward. Then a second and a third. The two of them moved deeper into the woods. Cain tiptoed around or hopped over as many dead sticks or piles of leaves as he could. Frank wasn't as nimble. His ankle slowed him down and limited where he could step. He pulled on low branches to help his balance as he limped along but seemed to snap every dry stick and crunch every dead leaf underfoot. Cain cringed at every loud noise.

Some engines at the homestead started up, at least one of the trucks and one, maybe two, of the bikes. It drowned out their steps a little, so Cain wanted to get as deep into the timber as they could while they had it as cover. He hustled forward to scout as clear of a path for Frank as he could find, then turned back to help Frank along.

The engines drew closer.

The noise peaked as they raced by on the road, now a few hundred yards back. Suddenly the bikes stopped, idled for a second, then the engines shut off. This time he was sure he counted two. Cain heard the truck continuing on, but the bikes were close.

"Crap."

The clouds had grown thick and dark; they cast a shadowy darkness in the woods. It helped, but Cain knew they were easy targets if those guys came after them right now. Searching for anywhere to hide, he spotted a pile of dead trees and brush about fifty yards ahead. Not ideal, but at least they could use it as cover. Its base was a huge oak tree whose branches had broken and collapsed on top of it since its demise.

He helped Frank hobble behind it, then helped him to the ground. He leaned up over the trunk and peeked through the tangle of branches. He could see well enough to shoot through it if he had to. With some luck, maybe it wouldn't come to that.

Cain slid down and leaned back against the huge old oak, thankful for a breather. Frank's face was nearly completely black from the dirt, dust, and dried blood on it, his chest covered in dirt and dead leaves that adhered to the sticky drying residue left over from his blood-soaked shirt. He picked at the leaves stuck to him.

"No, wait, leave those," Cain said. "It's like a little camouflage. Your white skin won't show up quite as much. How's your leg?"

"It hurts," Frank said, rubbing it.

"Keep an eye out that way. Let me see what I can do," Cain said.

He pulled up Frank's pant leg and slipped off his shoe. He didn't know much first aid, but that mix of colors had to be bad news. He pushed on it in different spots and rotated it slowly, watching to see where Frank winced. As far as he could tell the pain was worse side-to-side. He grabbed a couple of thicker sticks and pulled his shirt off. He tore off the sleeves and used them to tie the sticks as tight as he could get them to either side of his brother's ankle.

"It's not perfect, but it should help keep you from making it any worse," Cain said. "At least until we can get out of here." He tried to sound reassuring but felt like he sounded scared.

They heard the Ravens starting to move into the woods. These guys certainly weren't the ones that had been following them on the other side of the road. They were anything but stealthy. Their heavy footsteps sounded like there were ten or more men back there, but Cain knew on two bikes there was at most four. But four heavily armed Ravens would be more than enough to overpower him and a gimpy Frank.

You could just take off and leave Frank. You know, the way you left Gordon.

"We know you're in here," one of the guys yelled. "Just make it easy on yourself and come out. If we have to come after you, it ain't gonna be fun!"

"Well it might be fun for us," another other guy said.

They were still a good distance away and sounded like they might be heading in the wrong direction. Hopefully, they saw Frank's shirt across the road and bought the ruse. Cain took a deep breath and slowly blew it out. He looked for anything nearby that might put a little distance between them and the Ravens but still provide some cover.

"Hey, I see something," Frank said.

Too late. They were going to have to make their stand. This old dead tree was going to be their Alamo.

They actually fought at the Alamo. You don't. You hide. You're a chicken shit.

Cain ignored the voice in his head and peered up over the thick trunk, easing the gun out. Two figures, armed with rifles, moved in and out of the trees. They were young. Cain would have thought they might be new recruits except one had the Raven patch on his vest, so he was a full member. The other one had the probationary stripes on the back of his vest and looked like he was trying to grow a beard but little more than some dark fuzz had come in. He was a definitely a raw recruit.

Recruit was the wrong word; it wasn't like a boy had a choice on whether or not to join. At seventeen, boys were required to report to the Ravens for evaluation. The fortunate ones stayed and were trained as Ravens. The rest got sold to the farms as slave labor, and the farms were a living hell. The few men that Cain had met who had been released from service on the farms were damaged physically and mentally. He vowed to prevent that from happening to anyone that he could. Especially Frank, no matter how much he hated his brother on any given day.

Yeah, you sentenced Gordon to life at the farms because you were too scared to fight.

This kid looked fresh out of his evaluation and on his first mission with his supervising member. He probably heard the stories of the horrors that happen on the farms and was fearful of screwing up his first mission and getting sent there.

Cain knew that he had to kill them before they killed him and took Frank.

"Just come out! You can't escape. Poe survived your attack," the patched one said. "Once he's conscious, he'll send every man possible at you. We'll find you. We control everything for hundreds of miles. You aren't getting away. There's nowhere to--"

BANG!

Cain fired. The elder guy stumbled backward into a tree and slid down the trunk clutching his stomach; dark red streamers of blood flowed between his fingers. The fuzz-faced kid dropped to the ground, fumbling at a shoulder holster. Once he had gotten his pistol free, he fired a couple of shots in the boys' direction without aiming, then tried to roll behind the tree to use it and his partner's body as cover. Doing that completely exposed his profile.

"Dylan. Dylan. Stay with me buddy," the kid said as he quickly tried to feel for a pulse. His voice was high, and fear dripped from each word.

The other guy tried to speak, but blood in his mouth garbled his speech.

"Geth... dose... uckin...kith," he said. His head drooped like he'd dozed off under a shade tree in the summer.

Cain swore under his breath, steadied the sight on the kid's rib section, and pressed his finger to the trigger but eased off before pulling it. The kid was so young, and obviously had no training yet, but they sent him and his boss into the woods to possibly get slaughtered. Cain lowered his weapon and ducked behind the deadfall.

"Hey Peach Fuzz, don't be stupid!" he yelled, again aware of how high pitched his own voice was. "I'll kill you just like I killed your buddy. I've got the shot and coulda already killed ya if I'd wanted to. I'm giving you a chance to live. Just keep your back turned and don't follow us! You don't have to die for them!"

Frank had turned his back to the deadfall and pulled his knees up. He was muttering something Cain couldn't hear.

"Chance to live? Bull crap! They'll kill me if I don't bring you back," Peach Fuzz replied. "Or do worse than kill me. They're serious about getting you."

"No, they won't. They need loyal soldiers. Drag your buddy's body out of here and say he was still alive and you were trying to save him. They won't kill you. But I will if I have to!"

Peach Fuzz was silent for a long time. Cain peered over the tree and aimed the gun again. The kid had his back to the other tree, almost exactly back to back with his partner with the tree between them. Cain could see one shoulder and tell it was heaving up and down as the kid breathed fast and deep.

"Okay, go!" Peach Fuzz shouted, standing up, and holstering his gun.

"Stay down," Cain whispered to Frank. He tucked his .45 away and stood too, showing his empty hands. The two sized each other up for almost a full minute before Cain spoke.

"You could run too," he said.

Peach Fuzz hung his head and shook it.

"No, I can't. They'll kill my family if I run. They told us that Day One."

Cain nodded. "Yeah, they killed our family. I get it."

No, they didn't. You killed your family. >

Cain forced the voice out of his head. He climbed over the deadfall and walked toward Peach Fuzz, extending his hand; the other boy stepped forward and took it.

"Name's Jovi," Peach Fuzz said, somewhat of an embarrassed smirk crossing his face. "Yeah, mom was a Bon Jovi groupie back in the day. You know, before all the shit started."

"Cain? Can we go back and get Momma now?" Frank yelled from behind the deadfall.

Cain cringed. "My brother is, you know... kinda slow," he said. He turned toward his brother. "No, Frank. The bad guys are back there."

The bad guys? Who is the one who shot his precious Momma?

"Isn't he a bad guy?" Frank asked.

"No, he's not a bad guy," Cain said making eye contact with Jovi. "The Ravens are making him do things he doesn't want to do. He wants to come with us."

"I can't. I can't abandon my family to those psychos."

See. Some people protect their family instead of killing them.

"You can. I'll get you to some people who can protect you and your family."

"That resistance movement? No way. They aren't organized enough, or enough of them, to be any real threat to the Ravens. I mean, look, they couldn't protect you and your brother before this, how you think they'll be able to do it now that every Raven for miles is looking for you? Your best bet is to get as far out of Raven territory as you can. Plus rumors are that they just made a deal to get some new weapon to make sure that any resistance movement doesn't get off the ground."

"The resistance is gaining strength. They just need a leader--"

"That can make everyone believe--a guy with charisma. They want their own Poe. That guy can give his speeches and make you feel great. Until you realize that he's just using you to get power. Be the same way on the other side."

"We've got a bunch of safe houses that they can hide you until they can get you out of the territory."

"We? So you're officially part of them?"

"I've helped them. That's why the Ravens came looking for me in the first place. But--"

Jovi shook his head. "The guy you killed over there is Garcia's best friend. You killed another guy. Garcia and Poe are hurt bad. Poe might not make it. If I run, there's no way they won't kill everyone I've ever talked to. No way your people can get my family out before Garcia gets to them. Dude's crazy A.F."

Killed two men and one Momma! Score three!

Cain nodded. "Okay."

"Once I drag his body out, you know they're gonna send a whole unit in here looking for you two, right?" Jovi said. "They're not gonna screw around."

Cain sighed and looked at the dead kid slumped against the tree. "We need to make this look realistic, for your sake," Cain said, backing away. "We need to each fire off a couple of shots, so they'll hear it."

Jovi nodded and un-holstered his pistol again, making sure to point it in the opposite direction; Cain did the same. Jovi fired first, then Cain fired off two shots. Jovi fired another round.

A motorcycle engine roared.

"Shit!" Cain said. "Frank, run!"

Cain scurried back around the deadfall where Frank was struggling to his feet. Cain looked over his shoulder. Jovi was grabbing his partner under the shoulders. Cain nodded toward him; Jovi returned the gesture.

"Let's go, Frank. As fast as you can."

Chapter 9

The truck raced along the rough gravel road. Garcia felt every bump all the way to his teeth. He couldn't remember ever experiencing pain like this. Just when he had thought that it was becoming bearable, he went and stepped down on it trying to teach that probie a lesson. Now, every bump was making him hate the kid more.

The kid was going to be a bust anyway. Some were just too soft for the way the world was now. Working under his dad, he'd helped build the Ravens from a few preppers into something that resembled a functioning government. He had to learn how to size people up quickly. His dad called it knowing how to separate the wheat from the chaff. Essentially it was knowing how to tell the strong from the weak, those that were dead weight from those that could help them, those that could be Ravens from those that needed to go to the Farms. He'd learned that some people weren't worth the effort it would take to make them into a productive citizen, let alone a strong man. The Jovi kid fell into that category. The way he was so cocky sliding the magazine in and out of his Glock, but then looked like he wanted to faint when he heard a man choking on his own blood. Kid would never have the balls to make a difference. He wished he'd ordered Dylan to take him out once they got into the woods.

Poe gurgled and wheezed. His body seized then relaxed again.

Garcia squeezed his hand. "Remember when I was twelve and wanted to quit football because getting hit hurt too much. You wouldn't let me. You made me stick with it, and I ended up with a college scholarship. It worked out. Now I'm making you stick with it, and its gonna work out. You hear me. No options. You are going to live. And it's going to work out. We'll make those sons-a-bitches pay."

Back in the day, his dad's group of friends were scoffed at, told they were crazy, needed tinfoil hats, and countless other derogatory jabs, but it was their dedication to preparing for an apocalyptic scenario that allowed them to quickly establish some semblance of control with as little bloodshed as possible. He established rules that brought order out of the chaos. He established trade with neighboring groups that brought in things like gas, cigarettes, and alcohol. Folks in the middle of what used to be America wouldn't have any other way to get stuff like that. But still, not everyone respected the importance of having those rules in place. Some people were selfish. And those people needed to be made an example of. Those brothers were going to be an example for a lot of people.

The truck slowed and pulled to the side of the road.

Garcia tried to get his bearings. They weren't at Nevermore. The dust cloud swirled around him making it hard to spot any landmarks. He had no idea where they were. Why did this kid stop the truck? Was this some kind of trap? Between the darkness from the building storm and the dirt hanging in the air, he couldn't see more than ten yards. Thunder clapped and rolled for what seemed like minutes. He couldn't hear if someone was moving toward the truck. A chill ran down his back. His heart started to pound making his leg throb even worse. He reached up and banged cab's sliding back window with the butt of the gun.

"What the hell you doing," he said when he heard the window glass open.

"Orders from Doc. He said to wait here, and he's sending a gunship to escort us. Said there's resistance activity and he doesn't want them to catch us unarmed."

Garcia willed himself to turn around. His leg sent waves up pain all the way up to his skull. The edges of his vision blurred for a second. Every nerve in his body felt like a lit fuse. He looked over his shoulder at his dad's bloody face and tried to ignore the pain.

"We aren't unarmed. You see this gun. This says we aren't unarmed. Now I'm telling you that you need to go. Poe is dying back here."

"Doc said--"

The kid's words were cut off by the screen being punched out and the barrel of a gun pressed against the back of his head.

"What's your name, probie?" Garcia said through gritted teeth.

"Jordan, sir."

"Jordan, if you want to live to see tomorrow, you better do what I say."

"I understand, sir, but Doc outranks you. And his orders were to--"

The roar of the gun was deafening in the enclosed cab. A splash of blood and brains smacked into the windshield and dripped on the dashboard. Jordan slumped forward into the steering wheel.

"Son bitch. Look what you made me do!"

Garcia used his hands to push himself along the truck bed, then eased himself down on his good foot. He hopped along the side of the truck and pulled the driver side door open. He grabbed Jordan's body by the arm and pulled, sending it tumbling onto the gravel. He landed on his back with his legs bent back underneath him. A gaping red hole replaced what used to be his forehead.

"That little Jovi piss-ant would faint for sure if he saw this," he thought.

He backed up to the seat and used the blood-slicked steering wheel to pull himself into the cab. His sleeve served to wipe off the windshield; blood streaked across the spiderweb of cracks. Situating himself in the seat, he noticed there were three pedals.

"Jesus H. Christ! Can anything else go wrong!"

He snatched up an old paper towel from the console and stuck in his mouth. Biting down hard, he tried to press the clutch in with his left foot. Lightning flashed, and he wasn't sure if it was outside or from the pain. The lack of thunder and his rapidly hazing vision gave him the answer.

The radio crackled. Doc's voice filled the cab. "Jordan, your escort is about ten minutes from you, but you're gonna have to drive and meet up with them. Resistance is gonna beat them to--"

"Doc! Get 'em here faster. We're already taking fire!" He fired his pistol out the back window where the screen used to be into the empty road behind them. "Get 'em here!"

"Garcia? Where's Jordan? Where's--"

"Listen to me! Get those son bitches here now! Truck's a stick. I can't drive it, and they already shot Jordan. Get us the hell out of here."

Where's--"

RAT-Tat-Tat-Tat-Tat

The passenger window exploded. Bullets thumped into the side of the truck. Garcia dove down. His leg banged against the driver's door. The pain bolted so fast and hard that he gasped and his heart felt chilled in his chest. Blood warmed his cheek and dripped on the leather passenger seat.

Another round of fire echoed over the thunder. He heard the line of bullets thump along the door, just above his head. Doc had his guy, Biggs, install some scavenged armor plating along the sides of some of the trucks. He was suddenly thankful this was one of them.

He raised himself up enough to peer over the crystal barbs that were the remnants of the window. The wind was rushing through the window. The pain made his vision take on a surreal dream-like quality. The storm imposed darkness swirled and blended with the shapes of trees to make it look like an army was mere feet away. He concentrated but couldn't find any figures in the shadows.

Lightning flashed overhead, casting a little illumination on the scene. He spotted something roughly man-shaped. The figure raised the gun and fired.

RAT-Tat-Tat-Tat-Tat-Tat-Tat

Bullets thudded into the door. The truck rocked from the impact. One shattered the driver's window.

Lightning flashed, and the thunder followed immediately. He popped his head up. More lightning. This time, he clearly saw a man cast against the darkness. He fired off two shots. The man dropped, but he didn't know if he'd hit him or the guy tried for cover. Either way, it'd slow his advance a bit.

He pressed the button on the radio as another burst of shots hit the front of the truck. "You hear that Doc! Where the hell are your guys?"

He peeked again, found a target and fired. The lightning illuminating the guy's bloody neck as he collapsed told him that he'd gotten a kill this time. But he'd spotted at least two more out there.

His leg screamed in agony. But he ignored it and pushed himself up again.

RAT-Tat-Tat-Tat

The overhead console showered him with plastic shards. He fired twice. Missed. One guy ducked behind a wide tree about thirty yards away. Then he saw at least two, maybe three, more lagging a few yards behind. He fired three shots. One struck its target.

The guy behind the tree rolled out and fired off a round of shots. Garcia ducked as the truck shook again. When he raised back up the gunman was behind another tree ten yards closer. Garcia fired. Wood splintered, but no blood.

Two bright lights suddenly illuminated the scene as another truck rolled around the bend. Garcia raised his head to see if it was Doc's guys; he inhaled a deep breath when he saw 'Scarlett' painted on its side. Doc didn't just send 'a' gunship; he sent 'the' gunship to escort them. Doc had recently dealt for it in response to the increasing threat from the resistance; nothing like testing it out on some real targets.

THUNK... THUNK... THUNK... THUNK. The .50 caliber gun mounted on the back of the truck silenced the thunder and the smaller guns. It ripped off three more shots. THUNK... THUNK... THUNK.

They struck the man trying to take cover behind the tree. He all but exploded.

The euphoria of seeing that dulled Garcia's pain and allowed a smile to sneak across his face.

He was still watching what was left of the fighter rain to the ground when the driver's door swung open. He whipped around, gun pointed. His leg revolted against the sudden move, killing his buzz. Whiteness blinded him for a second or two. His heart felt like it wanted to stop.

"Whoa! Garcia! It's us!"

His vision cleared a bit, but the pain still was like a hard, electric shock through his body. He lowered his gun. He couldn't see who it was, but they knew his name.

The .50 caliber laid down another burst of fire into the field. He heard screams. He wanted to smile, but couldn't this time; his leg wouldn't allow it Those pigs deserved to suffer. He hoped that .50 cal ripped them open but just enough to keep them alive for a while. Long enough to know they were doomed. Long enough to feel the pain that their selfishness brought upon them.

"Can you move?"

Garcia shook his head.

Before he knew what was happening four hands had him and were lifting him out of the truck. A gunman ran in front of them firing into the trees to help provide some cover.

THUNK... THUNK... THUNK.

They slid him into the passenger seat on the gunship.

THUNK... THUNK... THUNK.

He startled at how the trucks shook when the massive gun let loose.

"Hang in there, man. We gotcha now. We'll get you out of here."

The white haze threatened to overtake Garcia's vision completely. "Wait," he said. "You gotta bring the other truck. Dad's in the back, and he's dying."

The driver shifted the truck into reverse but did a doubletake, unsure of what he'd just heard. "Yeah, we got the other truck too. Your dad's safe."

"Good," Garcia said. Then he let the whiteness take him.

Chapter 10

Cain and Frank moved through the woods as fast as Frank's bad ankle would allow. The hillside was steep, so their speed was curtailed by trying to maintain balance on the debris-filled ground. Branches and rocks rolled under their feet. Several times one or the other lost their balance and scraped up a knee or a hand trying to catch themselves. Every so often, they stopped for a few minutes so Frank could catch his breath and rest his ankle. He leaned on whatever tree was closest and panted. Sweat poured off him, mixing with the sticky blood residue on his chest.

Cain listened for sounds of anyone following them, but the only sounds he heard was the impatient thunder. Even the few birds that were chirping earlier had fallen silent. As they descended further into the ravine, the air became thick and still, enhancing the smell of the sweat and blood covering them. His stomach rolled.

"You stink," he said to Frank, hoping to ease some tension. "We gotta find shelter somewhere. It's gonna storm."

Cain jogged a few feet away and scanned the woods. He knew the area but hadn't been this deep into the woods in several years. He tried to spot a rock overhang, a shallow cave, or even another huge deadfall, anything to provide them some a little protection from the acid rain. It wasn't as acidic as the first couple of years after Impact, but on occasion, it was still bad enough to burn your eyes. Cain didn't want to take the chance that this would be one of those times. He strained to see into the shadows. His pulse quickened when he saw it.

About a third of the way up, a beat up little building emerged from the rolling hillside like some strange growth. It might once have been some kids' playhouse or fort or something. Whatever it was, it might work to hide under while the storm blew through.

"Frank, look here. Does that look like a little shack over there?" he said, pointing toward the other side of the ravine.

Lightning flashed, giving him enough light to feel confident it wasn't a mirage. His hope grew stronger by the second.

The momentary light had made it clear that it was a building of some kind. He prayed it was an old playhouse of some kind because the only other reason Cain could think someone would do that would be as supply storage. The possibility made him hopeful and fearful. Hopeful because it probably contained food and water, and he suddenly realized how hungry and thirsty he'd gotten. But fearful because no one would leave valuable supplies unguarded.

Thunder crashed above them.

When it died out, some dead branches snapped behind them. Cain pulled out his gun and whirled around. A gray wolf and two pups stood there. The mother stood about three feet tall but was very thin. She was missing patches of fur along both flanks, and one eye bore the telltale signs of acid rain exposure. She was missing most of one ear, and her snout was scarred. She stepped backward a step, arched her back, and bared her yellow teeth. Her right front paw tapped the ground, like a nervous student waiting for test results.

"Don't shoot!" Frank yelled. "It's just a momma woof and her babies. They want some food. They're hungry. She's just takin' care of them the way Momma took care of us." Groaning, he bent down to one knee and held out his hand. Cain could tell by the cracking in his voice that he was either crying or about to cry.

The mother wolf tapped at the ground and snarled. She took three steps sideways. The pups followed her lead.

"Frank, they smell the blood on you. You're the food they want. That's what we've been hearing, them tracking us. I gotta shoot her."

Just like you shot his momma. Shootin' mommas, it's what you do!

Frank stepped in front of the gun. "You can't. Just shoot some food for her to feed the babies."

"If there's a mom, there's a dad around somewhere--"

The wolf charged, snarling. Saliva dripped off her teeth and strung out behind her, sticking in her mangy fur. She leaped, her front paws landing on Frank's back. She was only heavy enough to stagger him, causing him to stumble into the gun barrel. Cain started, nearly pulling the trigger on accident.

Would it really be an accident? C'mon who you kidding? You want him to be dead. Dead like his momma.

Frank raised back up; the wolf rebounded off his back. Her paws flailed in the air, seeking anything her claws could grip. One his found his back, puncturing a bloody cut from his shoulder blade to above his waist. The she-wolf landed on her side with a thunk and a yelp but scrambled to her feet without a pause. She opened her maw and latched onto Frank's calf. She jerked her head from side to side trying to rip the skin from the bone.

The wind picked up, and lightning flashed overhead. Thunder immediately followed, no longer distant and rolling, it crashed around them. Dry leaves swirled around the pups. They howled one after the other in a constant chorus, like a crowd cheering for a gladiator.

Frank wailed and punched at the wolf's head. She yelped and released, taking a couple of steps back. Frank bent over and grabbed his wounded calf. The wolf lunged again, this time biting down on his shoulder. Her teeth dug into him, blood poured from the wound, the taste of it fed her intensity. She snarled and shook her head violently. Her claws tore at his back and legs trying to find the leverage needed to rip with her teeth.

Frank screamed. He couldn't maintain his balance and fell over backward, temporarily freeing himself from the snarling wolf. Before he could regain his footing, she was back on him. His blood dripped from her scarred snout as she tried to force her teeth toward his throat. He used his left forearm to hold her at bay; his right lie immobile and bleeding. Her glazed-over eye nearly even with his own, her back claws dug into the earth trying to hold her ground against his push. He swung his foot and caught one of her hind legs, dropping her, and momentarily pausing her attack. He wailed in agony because of the impact on his ankle.

BANG!

The report echoed through the trees, temporarily drowning out the howling pups and approaching storm. The mother wolf fell silent and collapsed onto Frank's legs. He clutched his right arm and screamed.

Cain dropped the pistol and squatted next to his brother; the wound was deep, but fortunately missed any major arteries. Frank gritted his teeth and panted, banging the back of his head into the ground and thumping one of his feet.

"Frank, I know it hurts, but we gotta get to that shelter before that rain cuts loose." Cain tried to lift his brother by his good shoulder, but Frank didn't budge. "C'mon, man. Listen to me!"

One of the wolf pups kept howling; the other snuck closer and was sniffing around its mother's body. He grabbed a stick and threw at the pup.

"Shoo! Get the hell outta here!"

Frank propped himself up, still panting through his teeth. He rolled to his knees, then collapsed back on his bottom, screaming in agony.

"Frank!" A raindrop struck Cain's arm, then a second. "The rain's starting!" Cain reached for his brother's hand to try to pull him up, but Frank ignored it. Another raindrop hit him. "Damnit! Get up, dummy, or I'm leaving you here!"

Frank tried to pull himself up but failed again, this time rolling completely to his back. Raindrops pelted him. Cain tried to boost him, but Frank was too heavy. Cain released his brother and ran several yards toward the shelter before turning back around.

Frank crawled to his knees, again. He put his good hand on a tree for balance as he swung his foot and planted it on the ground. He pushed up from that leg, clutching the tree. His face contorted in agony and he roared for a solid ten seconds as he forced himself, very slowly, to his feet.

Cain rushed back over and propped himself under Frank's functioning arm. "Good, Frank! Good!"

"Get... the... woofs," Frank said, still breathing through his clenched teeth.

Cain ignored him and kept moving forward. With each step, more drops pelted the boys and slicked the ground. His thighs burned from supporting Frank's bulk. Cain wanted to hurry before his small frame wasn't able to support the extra weight, but knew they had to be careful not to slip and send Frank tumbling onto that wounded shoulder.

"Cain, get the... babies."

"We don't have time to mess with that, Frank."

The wind whistled through the trees. Thunder clapped. The drops pelted them.

"We can't leave them... their momma's dead." Frank lifted his heavy arm off of Cain and turned around, taking a tentative hop back toward where the pups had curled up next to their mother's body.

Cain bolted to catch his brother, his knees still shaky from suddenly being unburdened. He tried to object, but Frank wouldn't relent.

"Fine, wait here," Cain said, motioning for Frank to stop. He sprinted over, picked both pups up by the scruff of the neck and carried them back. "The storm's getting bad, we have to get to that shelter. If I carry them, can you make it on your own?"

Frank nodded, blinking the rain out of his eyes.

Cain hurried down the hill and up the other side with the pups. By the time he reached the shelter, he was panting--hard. He wanted to collapse but knew he couldn't. Frank was still making his way toward the shack, wincing with every step.

Cain realized, for the first time, that he admired Frank's determination. He wasn't sure he wouldn't have given up if he were in Frank's shoes.

You know you would've given up. When they took Gordon, you hid. Frank's five times the man you are. Chicken shit!

Cain knew he had to figure out a way to get into the shed before Frank caught up. It was set into the side of the hill so only a little of it stuck out. Branches were nailed to it in a crude attempt at camouflage. The wooden door rattled against the beating wind, held shut with a hasp latch and a padlock.

Someone had tried pretty hard to keep it hidden. For a reason.

Cain kicked the door, busting the latch free. He set the pups down, then stepped inside, shaking out his hair and wiping the rain from his eyes. He glanced back; Frank was still moving steadily toward him.

The shed was lined with shelves, each loaded with supplies: gallon jugs of water, cans of soup, dried fruits and jerky, water purification tablets, a couple of backpacks, and a first aid kit. They'd just stumbled upon everything they needed to keep going as soon as the rain stopped. A supply stash like this was valuable; it wouldn't be unprotected. They wouldn't be able to stay here long. As soon as the storm broke, they had to get as far away as they could.

Frank's big body blocked the light coming through the door. Cain opened a jug of water and handed it to him.

"Here. Wash your eyes out good with this and then drink. I'll work on getting your shoulder bandaged as best I can. Whoever owns this place won't be far away," Cain said, already going through the first aid kit to see what he could use to bandage up Frank's wounds.

Frank took a couple long gulps of water, then poured some into his cupped hand and held it down for the pups to drink. He smiled as they slurped the water from his hand; when it was gone, he poured some more.

The smile disappeared when Cain began working on his shoulder. He jerked his hands away from the pups and yelled.

"I gotta bandage you up. Don't whine or I'll leave your ass here," Cain said.

Frank didn't speak but groaned and yelped a lot. After a few agonizing minutes, Cain had gauze bandages applied to both sides of his shoulder.

"That's as good as I can get it. Hopefully, we can find a doctor that isn't a Raven that'll look at you because you're gonna need more than I know how to do," he said, grabbing a jug of water and taking several drinks. He sat on the floor and watched the storm rage through the open door. Frank sat next to him with both wolf pups curled up on his lap asleep. "You know you have to leave them here--we can't take them."

"But, Cain--"

"No buts. We're gonna have to carry some of these supplies with us, and it's gonna be hard enough with you being all banged up. Plus, they've got a daddy that'll be looking for them, and we're out of bullets."

Maybe if you hadn't pumped two of them into your mom...

Cain shook his head and pushed the shaggy hair out of his face. Frank petted the animals asleep on his lap, a sad but peaceful look on his face. The sadness etched on Frank's face did nothing to assuage the guilt Cain was trying to force away.

"They'll die without their momma, Cain." Franks eyes filled with tears. "We can't let them die."

A thump on the roof followed by another thump, caused both boys to jump.

"Shit!" Cain said, springing to his feet. He reached for a water jug.

"Stop right there, kid," a voice growled. The business end of a shotgun lunged through the doorway. "H'nds up and turn 'round. You too, big boy, git up and keep your h'nds 'ere I can see, or I'll blow a hole right through ya."

Chapter 11

The man stepped into the shed, keeping his shotgun leveled at Cain's head as he did. He was stocky, with broad shoulders and stood about six feet tall. Water ran off the brim of his khaki safari hat like a waterfall, hiding most of his face, save for a thick gray mustache that ran all the way to his cheekbone. He wore a gray tank top, heavy work boots, and cargo pants that were threadbare and torn in several spots. He dragged on a lit cigarette clenched in one side of his mouth, then exhaled, sending smoke rolling out from under the brim between the serried drips.

"Whatcha boys doin' pokin' round my stuff?"

Cain hesitated, then said, "My brother is injured, and we got caught in the rain and needed a place to go." He kept his tone level despite his heart feeling like a bass drum.

Frank held his hands in the air but was still struggling to his feet. The pups shook themselves awake and started to paw on the dirt floor.

"Wrong wit' him?" The man said, nudging Frank's shoulder with the barrel of the shotgun.

Frank moaned and jerked his shoulder back.

"Eas' dere. No fast moves," the man said.

"Messed up ankle. Got attacked by a wolf. Lots of stuff." Cain nodded at the two pups.

The man's eyes widened, and he quickly looked at the animals, then back at Cain. Without moving the gun from his shoulder, he kicked the animals; both went airborne, one hit the doorframe, the other landed outside. The one that hit the doorframe lie unmoving on the ground. Frank bellowed something unintelligible and bent to get to the pup.

The man jumped back. He swung the stock of the shotgun around, bringing it to bear on Frank's temple. The crunch of the impact made Cain's stomach lurch. It seemed to echo off the walls, even drowning out the storm outside.

Frank dropped to the ground and didn't move.

Cain screamed and fell to the ground next to him. He felt around, trying desperately to find a pulse. "No! Frank! No!"

"Don't move 'gain er I'll blow <u>you</u> damn head 'ff. Hear me?"

Cain ignored him and kept feeling for any sign of life. "Frank!"--he shook his brother-- "Frank! C'mon, man!" Cain's chest tightened, and he had to force himself to take in a breath. He felt Frank's neck, nothing. Wrist, nothing. Heart, nothing. Finally, he brought his fist down hard on the bandaged shoulder. Frank's body went rigid, and he gasped for air.

"Oh thank God," Cain breathed and slumped against the shelves behind him. Frank moaned next to him, but between the moans, Cain could

hear that he was crying. He put his hand on
Frank's back and rested it there.

Chapter 12

A few hours later, the sun and yellowish haze had returned, bringing with it the staggering thickness of a rainforest. Cain looked at the sky; it didn't look like there was much chance of any relief from the pounding sun and stifling humidity. Bound at the wrists and ankles, they'd been baking in the back of the man's truck for the last thirty minutes. Frank sat silently across from him; his head hung and rested on his fists that were tight against his chest like he was praying. Either sweat or tears dripped from his face and ran between his fingers.

Cain started to say something but decided not to.

He heard the man trudging his way up the hill from the shed. The old guy wheezed badly, but it didn't stop him from smoking. He'd light one cigarette off the other. From ten yards away, Cain could hear his shallow wheezing breaths.

The man dropped two loaded backpacks into the passenger seat. He walked around and leaned on the tailgate.

"Comfy?" he said, looking at the sweat streaming down Cain's face. "Thirsty?"

Frank lifted his head and nodded. The man handed him a jug of water and three pieces of jerky.

"'Bout you?" he asked, looking at Cain.

Cain nodded. The man gave him the same. Cain gulped at the water and devoured one of the pieces of jerky. He was thankful for the food and water because they needed it, but more than that, it meant that the old man probably was not planning on killing them.

"We git movin' in a few m'nutes. Gotta get 'nother load."

"I could help you," Cain said. "You got my brother, so you know I won't run. Just let me out of these"--he showed his bound wrists--"and I'll help you carry stuff."

The man paused and blew out smoke. "I 'asn't b'rn yesterday, kid. Drink ya water 'n shut yer yapper."

Cain raised his eyebrows at his brother. Frank bowed his head and clutched his arms against his chest again.

Fifteen minutes later, Cain heard the old man's wheezy breaths coming up the hill.

"You still alive?" he said as he went by and deposited another two backpacks full in the passenger seat.

"What do you want with us? We didn't take anything except some water. Looks like you cleaned the place out, so we aren't gonna take anything else. Why are you keeping us here?"

The old man eyed Cain, lit another cigarette, and tossed the old one on the ground. He took off his hat and wiped his forehead with his sleeve. He replaced his hat and turned back around.

"Yer gonn' wanna hol' on," he said, climbing behind the wheel and revving the engine. He stomped on the accelerator, and the truck slid around the corner.

Cain and Frank both tumbled over. Frank's shoulder landed hard on the truck bed. He let out a groan, but pushed himself back up and resumed his pose.

Unsure if he should speak or not, Cain stared at his brother. After about twenty minutes of bumps along a road that hadn't been maintained in three years, the silence had begun to feel as heavy as the hot, humid air.

Cain sighed.

"I always resented you, even hated you a lot of the time," he said. "I always felt like Mom loved you more. You were her favorite. All I had was Dad, and that wasn't much. Then you even took that away from me. I hated you for it. Even today, part of me wanted to leave you in the woods, just leave you there and never look back." Tears bit at the corners of his eyes. "But back there a little bit ago, when I thought he'd killed you, I was scared, man. I was really scared. I'm so sorry."

Frank raised his eyes and met his brother's gaze. His eyes were bloodshot and puffy.

"It's okay, Cain," he mumbled.

It's not okay. He wouldn't say it's okay if he knew you killed his precious Momma, would he? You can try to make yourself believe it was an accident but was it really? He killed yours, so you killed his. That's how the game's played, right? You got your revenge!

"Frank, there's something else. I--"

The truck stopped abruptly. The truck door squealed open, and the shotgun quickly appeared pointed at Cain's head.

"Don' even think 'bout tryin' ta run," the man said. He dropped the tailgate and motioned for the boys to get out, then nodded at a German Shepherd sauntering toward them. "Maisey here'll catch ya 'fore ya got a hund'd yards."

The dog's ribs showed through her thin fur as she walked. Her eyes were milky and her teeth yellow, reminding Cain of the wolf. She started to lie down next to the man, but he kicked her. She yelped and slowly raised to her feet.

"Git up, ya l'zy bitch," he growled, taking off his hat and wiping the sweat from his brow. "It's hotter th'n a virg'n on prom night."

He untied their ankles and pushed them toward a set of rickety wooden stairs that led down to a dilapidated house. Some of the shingles were missing; the ones that weren't were faded and turned up on the edges. Two rusted, empty dog bowls sat next to a set of crumbling stone steps to the front door. One window on the west side was broken out and covered with plywood, but all the others were fitted with wrought iron bars.

The house sat lakefront, about fifty feet back from the shore. A gentle breeze disturbed the otherwise glass-like water. A wood plank walkway led to a small covered dock; a boat rocked gently in its slip. The idyllic setting clashed with the run-down house and its barred windows only a few feet away.

The man pushed them into the house while the dog moped a few steps behind. He leaned the shotgun against the wall and picked up a handgun from a table next to the door. He marched them into the living room. A stack of old magazines sat next to a stained steel blue chair. An ashtray overflowed on the magazine pile. The air smelled like fish and stale cigarette smoke. Empty beer cans rattled around their feet as they trudged through.

They went down the stairs to the basement. The man turned on a single bulb hanging from the ceiling. The basement, like the shed, was lined with supplies, neatly arranged on shelves. A sink stood in the corner, red stripes of what looked like blood streaked the basin.

He turned knobs to open deadbolts on a heavy metal door. Before unlocking the third, he wedged his foot against the door and chambered a round in the gun. He quickly turned the knob. The door swung back at him. It banged into his shoulder, but he had braced for the impact. A tall skinny man tried to force his way out. The old guy pressed the pistol against his forehead.

"Don' do it, Peters. You wo'th 'bout the same dead or 'live," the old man said, pushing the gun forward. Peters relaxed, holding his hands behind his back, but didn't back up. "Get your hands up, mother--"

"Or what, Taggart? Do it then! If you're gonna shoot me, do it! You ain't got the guts to do it, or you would've by now. You're worthless." Peters backed up and leaned against the wall.

The old man pulled the gun back and waved it at the brothers. "Yeah, I meh be w'rthless, but you ain't. You w'rth quite a bit. Now, ya two, git in 'ere. Peters won't be 'round much long'r, then ya 'ave the place to ya-selves."

The room was roughly a fifteen-foot square with a small adjoining bathroom. The pale blue paint was chipped off in several spots and completely scrubbed away in some others. The bathroom had no door, just a toilet, sink, and a garden hose to serve as a makeshift shower. A double bed with no sheets stood against one wall. Next to it was a barred egress window with a view of the boat dock and the lake. The glass had been removed, and the stifling air blew in from outside.

"I'm g'nna drop pair of scissors o'er dere so that youc'n cut off those ties. Then ya put the scissors outside 'n da groun'. Ya ain't gittin' no food 'til those scissors're outside. Clear?"

"Taggart, who's looking for these guys?" Peters said. He had fiery orange hair that contrasted with his pale skin. The last remnants of a black eye begged for notice around his right eye and light glared of his oily forehead. He wore shorts and was shirtless; though his arms were thin, his core looked strong. He wasn't starving, so the man must've taken decent care of him.

"Nobody. Caught 'em raidin' one a my supply caches,"--the old man nodded toward Frank--"an' a big boy like dat w'rth a lotta money to da farmers."

"Not unless he gets some medicine for his arm. That wolf bite is bad. He ain't worth squat with one arm," Cain said.

Frank's eyes grew wide, and his face lost its color. "Cain, are they gonna cut off my arm. I don't want them to cut my arm off, Cain."

"Shhh, Frank. No, they're not going to cut your arm off, but if you don't get some medicine, it won't heal right and be as strong."

"I ain't gittin' no doctor out 'ere. I'll get ya some alc'hol and clean b'ndages. Fix'm up best ya can. As long as they buy, I don' give a crap if it don' work once they gone. They'll think they're gettin' a deal an'way, twofer price a one,"

The man backed out of the room. The gun swung back and forth as if scanning each of the captives. The door shut and the three bolts slid into place. Cain knew it was hopeless but yanked on the door handle anyway. A couple minutes later, the man's boots appeared outside the window and dropped a pair of scissors on the ground.

"Back 'ere or ya ain't gittin' fed."

Peters walked over and reached through the bars to retrieve the scissors.

"This guy has a room with bars on the windows and locks on the doors, what the hell?" Cain said, holding his arms out so Peters could cut him free. He took the scissors, cut Frank free, and tossed them out the window as instructed. "Who is he, and why'd you ask who was looking for us?"

"William Taggart the Third. He was a drug dealer before the Impact. Now, he's a bounty hunter. Figured if he was stashing you in his little dungeon, that you must be wanted by somebody."

Cain pulled on the window bars. They were solid, too.

"What's he got you for?"

Frank stared out the window. "Maisey. Come here, girl," he said, holding his hand between the bars.

"I wouldn't mess with that dog. He don't feed her, so she's mean," Peters said. Then he paused and smirked as if relishing some nostalgic memory. "Freakin' Ravens. Who else? One of them owed me for some *goods* I got for him. He tried to weasel on the debt. Ran into the guy at-- how old are you? Never mind, you're a kid--ran into him at an *establishment*. Kicked his ass pretty good. Three of them showed up at my house later, only one went home. Hence, there's a supposedly a big bounty out for me. Taggart thinks he's gonna be set for a year from turning me in. I've been here a week, and no one's showed up to collect me yet. Guess I'm not that valuable after all."

"Why aren't you trying to find a way out of here?" Cain asked, looking around the bathroom for any kind of loose wall panel that he could pry open.

"Why? He's got this place more secure than Alcatraz was back in the day. You think I haven't looked? I spent my first couple days here frantically trying to find an escape. But it's hopeless. You're wasting your energy."

Cain ignored the advice and kept looking.

Maisey plodded over to the window and sniffed at Frank's hand. Her bony back arched up, and she lowered her head and growled. Frank didn't pull back.

"It's okay girl, I not gonna hurt you."

Cain sighed and ran both hands through his stringy black hair, flopping it out of his eyes. "Frank, will you quit messing with that damn dog and help me find a way out of here!"

"Good girl," Frank said, as Maisey laid down just beyond his reach. "Sorry, Cain. What you want me to do?"

Cain sighed and slid down the wall until he sat on the ground. He ran his hands through his hair again. Frank stood there looking at him. Blank. Innocent. He knew this was how the rest of his life was going to be. He was going to be the one that needed to give Frank all the answers... all the comfort... all the praise.

Your fault. This is all your fault. No one to blame but yourself.

"I have to think a while. Just do what you want for a while. Okay? Go ahead and talk to the dog if you want," Cain said to Frank.

Frank nodded and went back to look out the window.

Peters stretched out on the bed. "Told you, there's no way out."

Cain looked over at Peters lounging on the bed. "Why aren't you worried? They're going to kill you. Probably already killed your family. And you act like you're at some vacation place."

"Resort? Is that the word you're lookin' for? I was worried the first couple of days. But like I said, after a week I know that killing me isn't a priority. I'm pretty confident that with my connections on the outside, that I'll be able to get their hands on enough stuff to make them see my value."

"What kind of stuff?"

"You name it, and I've got contacts that can get it. Alcohol, drugs, information, weapons. Pretty much anything."

Cain studied Peters. During the last year, he'd spent a lot of time in the shadier parts of the market and didn't remember anyone that looked like him. He thought he'd remember that fiery red hair. He could have been in disguise, but he seemed like the type that wanted people to recognize him. The kind that wanted to be remembered. Wanted to be infamous.

"So, you're a scavenger?"

"Little more elite than that. Scavengers will do anything. I only deal in illicit goods. The more illegal, the higher the price."

The slight about scavengers sent a moment of anger rushing through Cain. While it was true that he'd go searching for legal goods too, he didn't see that as a bad thing. Not everyone had the time or ability to go digging through empty homes and businesses looking for items that could be sold in the market. Admittedly legal goods weren't as lucrative as the illegal stuff, but the quantity he could move helped him feed Frank and his mom. Frank wouldn't have understood, but she had to know how he was earning the seeds, meat, and bread he brought home. Since she never so much as asked a single question, he took that as an implicit approval. If she approved, he really shouldn't care what someone like Peters thought, but it did.

Like you cared whether she approved or not. Since when did you listen to her. If she told you to stop, you would have tried to sell double.

He pushed the voice away and paused so the flash of anger could ebb. "So when you said 'an establishment,' you meant the Crease. I used to do some business in the market, both above and below ground. I know a few dealers down there. Don't remember ever hearing about you," Cain said, convinced Peters was bluffing about being some high-end scavenger.

"You know the Crease, huh? You seem kinda young to be hanging out in the Crease. So, I guess you know Davey Benoit? Angel?"

"Yeah. Done business with both of them," Cain said, hoping the lie wasn't obvious on his face. It was true that he'd done a fair bit of business with Davey Benoit, but he had no idea who the Angel person was. He couldn't even remember having overheard the name.

"You saying you're a scavenger?" Peters said.

"I am. Sold 'em both all kinds of stuff. You're nuts though if you think Davey will hook you up with guns to feed to the Ravens. He hates the Ravens. You better have some other contacts if you think you're gonna save yourself that way."

"Ahhhh! You're the kid scavenger that Davey used to rave about. You'd have thought you're his son the way he bragged about how good you were."

"How good I *am*. I'm not done yet," Cain smiled. He always like Davey. Sometimes dealers in the Crease thought they could take advantage of him because he was young. Davey never treated him like that. He also appreciated that David's hatred of the Ravens meant that any guns Cain sold him wouldn't find their way into Raven hands. It was good to hear the affection was mutual.

"Your name's Cain, right?"

"Yeah."

From where he sat on the opposite side of the room, Cain couldn't see the smile slither across Peters's face or hear him whisper "The infamous Skinny Cain. My get out of jail free card just arrived."

Chapter 13

Gabriel glanced nervously over his shoulders, then zipped up his sweatshirt. The lettering on the front used to read Lake Brenton Lakers in regal turquoise and orange letters, but now, they were cracked and fading. He pulled the hood up and forward so that it swallowed his thick gray hair and shaded his face. The shadows deepened the lines around his mouth and eyes. A cigar stump stuck out of his mouth and reflected on his steel colored eyes. He hated cigar smoke, but it helped shield his face a little, making it harder for him to be recognized. Men of God really shouldn't be noticed in places like the Crease.

After checking around him a final time, he muttered a quick prayer and slipped down an alley four blocks off of the Main Street Market. And the marquee that two of his friends and a third soul hung from. Every time he thought of it, the hate bubbled up. Hate for the Ravens and hate for the man whose jealousy had sent his friends to their graves. His heart was full of hate. Men of God shouldn't be so full of hate, he told himself. Hebrews 12:15 that cautions the faithful to watch that the poisonous root of bitterness is allowed to grow and trouble you and corrupt many. He prayed for strength but was afraid the root had found fertile soil in his heart.

He rounded a corner, trotted down a flight of stairs, opened a door and slid inside. On the other side was a long dark hallway. He followed it several hundred feet until it opened into a large, smoky room. The ceiling was low which trapped the smoke like a thick fog. The walls were about fifty feet on a side, lined with mismatched wood paneling that was popular in the 1970's. Undoubtedly, it had been scavenged from any number of mobile homes around the lake that once served as vacation homes for moderately affluent people from the cities. There were high-backed booths along the outer walls and some tables and chairs scattered about in the middle. Each table or booth had a candle or lantern, making the room fairly bright, but the thick smoke dulled the effect. About twenty people mingled around; some stood and talked, others huddled in the booths. There were open doorways on the walls to his left and right. Two closed doors on either end of the wall in front of him were separated by a long wooden bar.

The bottles behind the bar caught his eye. He forced himself to look away from them, but they drew his eyes back. It had been almost two weeks since he'd touched the stuff. He wanted to give in; he wanted a drink. 'Not today,' he told himself and moved toward the door to the left of the bar. The bartender intercepted him.

"Getcha something, pal?" he said, drying off a glass and setting on the bar.

Gabriel eyed the glass. His stomach could feel the scotch warm him from the inside out. At that moment, there wasn't a feeling he wanted more. It would relax him. Help him forget what he'd seen in the market. Help him have the courage to do what he'd come here to do. His eyes darted toward the door but returned to the bartender.

"Scotch. You got any ten year?"

The bartender shook his head. "Oldest I got at the moment is five."

"Fine," Gabriel said and leaned against the bar. His finger traced along the top, mahogany. It was beautiful, and he knew it well. It used to be the centerpiece of Fazio's Speakeasy, the best Italian restaurant on the lake. He'd been at Fazio's, seated at this very bar, examining the world through the bottom of a glass, when he decided to break his vow of celibacy. When it showed up here, he was convinced it was God's way of forcing penance on him. But he wasn't sure he was really sorry; he'd truly loved her. Guilt pecked at him for many of his failings, but Emily wasn't one of them. Her alone, he refused to ask forgiveness for.

He made sure his hood was tugged forward and puffed his cigar, watching his smoke mingle and disappear into the other haze.

The bartender sat the glass down in front of him and filled it. "That'll be about a quarter pound."

Gabriel took a sip of the scotch. Not bad, certainly not good enough to assuage his guilt about caving so easily, but good enough to do the job. He covered a packet of seeds with his hand and slid it across the bar.

"Here. And I want a pass," he said and nodded toward the door.

The bartender smirked, pulled a scrap of red paper from his shirt pocket, and handed it to Gabriel. "Give this to the guard. He'll show you the way. Unless you already know your way around." He smiled knowingly and winked.

Gabriel felt his face warm, uncertain if it was the scotch or the embarrassment. He swallowed his drink and thunked the glass back down on the bar. His throat burned as it rolled down. His muscles loosened, and he shut his eyes, relishing the feeling. Once it was gone, he tapped his finger behind the glass like a blackjack player asking for a hit. The bartender poured another, and Gabriel promptly threw it back and took a few moments to enjoy the way it made him feel. He'd deal with the penance later.

He dropped another package of seeds on the bar and went toward the door.

The other side was a short flight of stairs that ended at another hallway, this one guarded by a very large man dressed in all black, which made him hard to see in the dimly lit hall. Only a long gray beard and the sparkle of finely-honed blade gave him away. The guard pointed a gun with one hand and clutched the knife with the other.

"Got a pass?" he said. The tone of his voice affirmed he shouldn't be messed with.

Gabriel held up the paper from the bartender.

The guard lowered the gun and examined the pass. "Follow me," he said, tucking it into a shirt pocket.

Gabriel knew the way, but after the bartender's comment, he didn't feel like admitting it. The guard led him down the hall past several closed doors. When they stopped, the guard opened another door and motioned him inside.

The room inside was cavernous, like an old warehouse. It was lit only by a few candles, and large concrete pillars supported the ceiling twenty feet above. They cast long shadows that threw swaths of the room into near total darkness. Couches, beds, chairs, and other assorted furniture were scattered around the room. On one of the couches, a girl, not more than twenty, lie motionless with a needle still stuck in her arm. Her long red hair hung over her face. Gabriel's breath stuck in his throat. He approached her and said a prayer of thanks when he got close enough to see it wasn't his daughter. Then he bent, pulled out the needle, and felt for a pulse. Nothing. A little respite from this hellish world had cost this woman her life; he prayed she was in a better place.

About two-hundred people mingled around the room. They huddled in pairs or trios making deals. Deals that brought pleasure, deals that brought pain, deals that, in some cases, meant the difference between life and death. The Lake Brenton black market sold everything that was illegal to buy in the Main Street Markets: alcohol, drugs, weapons, and sex. The Ravens got their cut via the sale of passes, so they looked the other way and let people have their escape from reality. But since weapons were involved, he was convinced that they had spies down here to keep tabs on who was buying what and to snatch up anything too powerful that might be changing hands.

He blew out smoke from his cigar and scanned the room. He found who he was looking for on the far side. Two women waited there, white gossamer gowns displaying their bodies. One had long, dark hair and wore an old set of costume angel wings that were missing at least half the feathers; those that remained were closer to dingy gray than white. When he approached, she stepped forward and ran her hand down his bicep.

"Wanna ride to heaven?" she said.

The other woman leaned against a pillar and pulled her stocking higher on her thigh, causing her gown to fall open. The winged girl reached up and tilted his head down to draw his focus back. He made eye contact with her, then glanced at the other woman again.

"Oh, you want us both? I'm not sure you could afford it."

Gabriel leaned close to her. She wore perfume. He closed his eyes and breathed it in for a second. Something that once was so ordinary was now a luxury that few could afford. He moved closer to her ear and relished the way she smelled before he whispered to her, "We need to talk. Alone."

"Mmmmmmm," the woman purred in his ear and smiled, opening her neck up, so her perfume attacked his resolve again. She whispered, "She's fine. She's got no love for the Ravens." She pulled her face back, bit her bottom lip, and traced her finger down the zipper on his sweatshirt.

He nodded. She took him by the hand and pulled him back through the crowd. Once in the hallway, she released his hand, unlocked one of the closed doors, and followed him inside, locking it behind them. She lit a candle on a bedside table, illuminating a tiny room with a four-poster bed along one wall and small table and two chairs in the far corner.

"You've been drinking," she said.

He took a deep breath. "Yeah."

"You okay?"

He nodded. "Just two. I stopped, but I didn't want to."

She hugged him and held him for a long time. Her perfume did more to relax him than the scotch had. He wanted to stay here and let her hold him. Let her love him. But then he remembered why he'd come here and pulled away from her.

"I need to tell you something," he said, avoiding looking too long at the way the candlelight behind her gown made it virtually invisible.

"Okay?"

He took a deep breath. "Davey's dead, Angel. Beth is too."

Her face went blank.

"What do you mean? How?"

"Poe hung them in the market. Paul Fischbach ratted them out about D.J. not being sent for evaluation."

"You saw this?"

"Yeah, I was in my--"

"And you didn't do anything to stop it?" she said, her voice taking on a harsh, accusatory tone.

"Angel, I couldn't. What was I going to do? Start a gunfight in the middle of the market? What good would that do? I'd be dead too, but it wouldn't have saved them."

Tears streamed down her cheeks. Pangs of guilt struck him. He reached for her, but she turned away.

"You could've tried! He was your friend!"

"There's more. Paul told them that Davey did business with Skinny Cain."

She turned her head and leveled her gaze at him.

"Is that the kid?"

"Yeah."

"What is it with you and this kid? I told you he was trouble, but you didn't listen to me. You--"

"No, I didn't listen to you. I listened to God, and he told me that this kid is worth fighting for."

"Oh, he told you that did he?! I love how you pick and choose when you want to listen to what

God tells you. You want a drink, don't care what God says. You want sex, don't care what God says. You have a freaking kid, don't care what God says. But God tells you to trust some street-rat, and you're all about it no matter how many people you put at risk. Wake up, Gabriel! God doesn't exist. No benevolent god would create this hell of a world."

Her words hit him square in the gut. Since the Impact, he'd had those same doubts many times. Hearing her say the same thing felt like God calling him out for his weakness.

"Don't talk like that. Davey knew the risks. He died for our cause. He died a martyr."

"For shit's sake, Gabriel, he was your friend. How can you be so cold?" A fresh wave of tears took her. She covered her face and shook.

He reached for her but pulled his hand back.

"It's not cold. It's just the way things are. We can use the brutality of his death to try to sway people against the Ravens. I've spent all afternoon praying about this. God finally brought me peace and a clear vision forward."

Her eyes were red and puffy, and her mouth hung agape.

"You're a fool," she spat. "Unbelievable. Totally unbelievable. You watched your friend die and just shrug it off as a casualty of the cause. God damn you, Gabriel." She got up and opened the door. "Get out."

"Angel, listen--"

"Get out, or I'll signal the guard,"

Chapter 14

Cain struggled to get any rest on the hard floor. He tried to force himself to stay awake and find a way out of here, but eventually, sleep came, only to be haunted, restless, and short-lived. Each time he dozed off, he'd hear Gordon's pleas for help, or see the look of shock and fear on his mom's face when she realized that she was going to die, or her body laid out in the truck bed with Frank brushing the hair away from her eyes.

Frank seemed to have been awake most of the night too; he alternated between groaning or quiet sobs. The sound of Frank crying, alone in the dark, ripped at his heart. It was his fault they were in this predicament, and he didn't know what to do to make it better.

He slid over next to Frank who was lying on his back under the window.

"Not sleeping either, huh?" he said in a hushed voice.

"I miss her, Cain."

Cain sighed and leaned his head against the wall.

"If you shut your eyes and wish real hard, maybe she'll be alive again," Cain said.

Frank let out a tear-choked laugh.

"That's not true. I told you that when you were little so you wouldn't cry. It wasn't really true."

Cain smiled. "Yeah, I remember. I was little. Like what, nine or ten? I stole dad's pellet gun, and I killed that squirrel."

"You shot it right in the eye. Just like you said you were gonna do."

"I was so scared. Thought I was going to get my ass beat," Cain said, allowing himself to smile at the nostalgia.

"You cried a lot. If you didn't stop crying, we were both gonna get spanked."

"I still remember you saying, 'Cain, if you shut your eyes and wish real hard, maybe it'll be alive again. Now go over there and start wishing.' When you called me back over and told me it hopped up and ran away, I remember being so happy. I believed in that magic for the longest time. Frank magic, I called it."

Frank laughed again, this one a little less tear-choked.

"What did you do with it? I never asked," Cain said.

"Nothing. Told you. It was magic."

Cain glanced down and saw Frank's eyes were shut. He was smiling.

Feeling a little better, Cain drifted off, but it wasn't long before he was awoken by the clomp of boots outside the window.

"Git outta h're!" Taggart yelled. Maisey yelped, plodded over, and laid down by the steps. Peters and Frank both groaned and shook the sleep away. "H're's some food"--he put some sandwiches on the ground outside the window-- "an' some alc'hol and bandages. Get 'im fixed up 'nough ta be sold off, dat's all I care 'bout."

"Taggart," Peters said. "Hey, I want to write a letter to my wife."

"Ya don't need ta write no l'tter. Ravens gonna kill ya soon, anyway. She prolly th'nks ya already dead. Prolly not losin' no sleep over it, either."

"She's probably worried sick. If they're going to kill me when you hand me over, I want her to know what happened. What do you care anyway?"

"Fool, how ya gonna get it to her?"

"I'm sure the Ravens would happily track her down and give it to her. They'd love to watch her suffer when she reads my last words. They're sadistic like that."

Cain raised an eyebrow. For a guy that just a few hours ago was confident that he'd be able to talk his way out of his situation, he suddenly seemed resigned to the fact that he was going to die. Something wasn't right.

Cain's grandpa had spent his retirement at the poker tables all up and down the Vegas strip. As soon as Cain was old enough to count, Grandpa Ben was teaching him the fine art of playing poker every. He'd tell Cain, "The secret to winning at poker is not in getting good cards, it's all about being able to lie and know when the others are lying. Don't even look at your cards. Look at the people. If you watch close enough, they'll tell you if you can win or not. Everyone has a tell--a twitch in their eye, might wipe their nose, maybe look at the dealer. Everyone does something when they're lying. Watch for that, and it won't matter what cards you have." Cain never understood what he meant until now. Peters was lying about something. His attitude changed too fast.

Without another word, the old man walked away. Peters scrambled off the bed and snatched the sandwiches. He handed one to each of the brothers. Cain hesitated, unsure of whether or not he should trust the food. Peters swallowed his in about two bites.

"He wants us alive," Peters said, while still chewing the last bite of his sandwich. "More money that way."

"That so," Cain said.

"Come here, Maisey," Frank said, holding part of his sandwich out the window.

"Frank, what are you doing? You need to eat that. You need your strength to heal up," Cain said, still looking over his sandwich.

"Bett' listen to 'im," the old man said, stomping down the stairs from the porch. "Dat dog ain't gonna like ya no m'tter how much food ya give 'er. H're's paper an' a pencil."

Peters smiled and took the paper. He scribbled on it for a few seconds and handed it back to the old man.

"Damn fast l'tter," the old man said.

"Read it and see if it sounds good," Peters said, his face pressed through the bars.

The old guy walked away and then looked down at the letter.

Come get me out of here tomorrow to talk. I won't give you any problems... I got a business proposition for you. But we need to talk... alone.

Chapter 15

Garcia propped himself up on his wooden crutches and gazed down at his dad. He was sedated and sleeping as peacefully as he could with a broken nose, a jagged cut above one eye, a cracked rib, and three or four shattered teeth.

He shook his head. He'd argued with his dad before they left to ride out to that house about bringing guns. There was no logical reason to leave them behind, but his dad wouldn't hear it. "Take a knife if you want, and I've got my baton and whip. If I'm right, that's all we'll need." He wasn't right. And now he was bedridden, and those brothers were alive and running free.

"At least until Dylan catches up to them, then more than likely they won't be either," he thought.

"It's not as bad as it looks. He's going to be okay," Doc said, putting his hand on Garcia's shoulder. At six-foot-six, Doc stood a good six inches taller than Garcia. He was lean and muscular; he kept himself in great shape for a sixty-two-year-old. He had just enough razor stubble to seem rugged, but his well-coifed salt and pepper hair gave off a classy air. In the old days, he was always dressed to the nines, and still dressed well now. But now, his khaki slacks and pressed shirt seemed out of place in a world gone to hell.

"He'll have some scars. I don't have the kind of equipment I used to, ya know. But all things considered, he's fortunate. I vaguely remember his face looking this way once before." He laughed and walked to the other side of Poe's bed to check the IV drip.

Garcia had heard the story a million times about how his dad and Doc became friends. Doc worked in the ER at the university hospital and had been the one to do an emergency caesarian when Poe's wife's heart stopped during labor. Garcia survived; his mother didn't. Poe blamed the doctor. A year or so later, he and Doc ran into each other at a bar. Words were exchanged, followed by punches. Doc had Poe on the ground and was bloodying his face pretty good when a few other guys pulled him off. Doc held out his hand; Poe took it. They went back inside and drank together the rest of the night--despite Poe's bloody face and shirt--and had remained friends ever since.

Doc was the only person to beat Poe in a one-on-one fistfight, until yesterday. Doc was also the only other person that knew Garcia was Poe's son.

"When you get your head clear, we need to talk about what you told McCoy yesterday," Doc said.

Garcia turned toward him. The cold hand of embarrassment grasped him. He'd give up drinking eight years ago because he hated being told what he said and did the next day and not remembering any of it. Although this was a different situation, it brought back those same feelings. He strained his memory. The last thing he remembered was throwing that panty-waste Jovi kid against the truck then nothing until a short memory of driving down the road and the probie pulling off to the side.

"What're you talking about?"

"You're all hopped up on painkillers right now. We can talk later."

"No, you know how I feel about not remembering stuff. I'm fine. Just tell me."

Doc sighed and motioned toward the door. They stepped out of the room, and Doc shut the door behind them.

"He might be in and out of semi-consciousness, and I didn't want him to hear this and get alarmed." Doc took a long deep breath before continuing. "When our guys got there, you and your dad were in the back of a truck that was under pretty heavy fire from resistance fighters, do you remember that," he said in a very calm and slow manner.

Garcia looked scared. He felt scared. And his patience was running thin for Doc's reluctance to spit it out. He shrugged and raised his eyebrows as if to say 'what's your point?'

"You said, on the radio, that your driver got shot. We recovered the body. He'd been shot in the back of the head from point-blank range. You killed one of our own men."

Garcia felt anger surge up in him.

"No. No, I didn't. The resistance bastards shot him."

Doc leveled his gaze. "No, they didn't. They were firing from your three o'clock. He was clearly shot in the back of the head. His forehead was missing, Garcia. It was you. It could only have been you. And McCoy said that you seemed alert sometimes and other times you fell unconscious. But when you were alert you said that if that goddamned probie had listened to you, then you wouldn't have had to kill him."

Garcia's vision blurred as the rage boiled over. He shoved Doc against the wall. One of his crutches fell to the floor, sending him askew. Doc grabbed him by the shirt and kept him from falling, then pulled him closer.

"Don't test me, boy. I bested your old man, I sure as hell can best you," Doc said, the menace clear in his voice. "Now get yourself under control."

Doc bent over to pick up the fallen crutch. When he was bending down, Garcia used his other crutch to push him over. Doc hit the floor face first and instantly rolled to his back. Garcia hopped a step forward and lunged with the crutch so that its foot stopped not more than an inch short of Doc's throat. Doc's eyes bulged in surprise.

"I ain't my old man, and you ain't young anymore. I could've killed your old ass right here. Don't forget it."

Doc pushed the crutch away from his throat; Garcia didn't resist. He grabbed the second one, pushed up, and handed it back to Garcia.

"As if your dad isn't going to have enough to worry about when he gets back on his feet without having to try his own son for treason--"

"He's not gonna have to do shit. McCoy'll keep his mouth shut. I'll make sure of it," Garcia said. His chest heaved up and down with each breath as adrenaline surged through his body. He glared at the older man.

"Oh, yes, he's going to have to address it. Because you also told McCoy that Poe's your dad. And keeping secrets wasn't McCoy's strong suit. So, it's spread like wildfire. I've heard the whole story from at least four guys. I tried to play it off as you having semi-conscious hallucinations from the extreme pain. But they're going to believe McCoy's story, they all saw Jordan's body when--"

"Who's Jordan?"

"Your driver. The probie with half a face left. There wasn't any doubt McCoy was telling the truth about that, so if that was true, why wouldn't the rest be true too. Poe's going to have to take a stand, or it'll look like he's playing favorites with his son. It'll weaken his position with the men... and the public."

Garcia felt numb. He stared at Doc but couldn't formulate any words.

"I tried to mitigate the damage as best I could by having McCoy reassigned to the farms. Since he's not here, he won't be able to testify against you directly, but since so many people know, your dad will have to provide some sort of retribution. Without McCoy, though, you won't be sentenced to death." Doc stepped toward Garcia and pushed him gently against the wall. "I saved your life... for now... but McCoy could reappear. I hold your life in my hand. Don't forget it."

The rage bubbled in Garcia again, but he forced himself to hold it in check.

"Did they get those two brothers?" he said, trying to change the subject.

Doc shook his head.

"Goddamnit! You've got to be kidding me? Dylan was out there. He's the best I've ever seen at tracking freaking deer. The clod of an older brother shoulda been a piece of cake to follow. Where's Dylan? I want to talk to him."

Doc was silent.

"What? Where is he?"

"There was a shootout between the brothers and Dylan and Jovi. The brothers escaped."

Garcia unleashed a guttural scream and punched the wall, knocking a hole in it.

"That's not all,"--Doc paused and took a breath--"Dylan's dead. He got killed in the shootout."

Chapter 16

Frank stood at the window, his face pressed between the bars. "Maisey, Come here, girl." The dog sauntered over but eyed him warily. He set a piece of sandwich on the ground. The dog sniffed it, then scooped it into her mouth. Frank smiled and put another piece on the ground. "Good girl," he said.

"If you're gonna waste good food on that mangy dog, let me eat it," Peters said.

Frank took a bite and laid another piece on the ground, closer to the window this time. The dog watched Frank but stepped closer. Taggart dropped something upstairs, and the sudden sound frightened the dog; she slunk backward, growling.

"It's okay, girl. I won't hurt you."

"You really are simple or something, aren't you, pal?" Peters said.

"Don't talk to him like that!" Cain shot back.

"Easy, buddy. I didn't mean anything by it. It's just that we get so little food for us, it's certifiable to give it to some dog."

"Frank, you need to eat your food. You need it."

"But Cain, she's starving. I can share."

Peters shook his head and shrugged.

"Frank is a gentle giant. He loves animals. He tried to stop me from shooting the she-wolf that ripped up his shoulder."

He wasn't so gentle when he was punching your dad so hard it killed him, was he? But it's okay, you got even. You kill mine, I kill yours. That's how this game works!

"See. He's certifiable. The farms will want their money back from him. Actually, they probably won't bother. They'll just put a bullet in his head and save themselves the hassle."

Frank turned around. His face was frozen in fear.

"Cain, I don't want to go to the farms."

"You aren't. I'm gonna get us out of here. You trust me, alright?" Cain said, glaring toward Peters who stretched out on the bed, his fingers laced under the back of his head like he was lounging on the beach.

Gordon trusted you, look how that turned out for him.

Frank still had a look of terror etched on his face.

"Frank, you gotta trust me. I'll figure something out."

Frank nodded and turned back to the window.

"You're almost as crazy as he is. If I told ya once, I told ya a million times. There's no way out of here. Might as well relax and hope the old bastard keels over or something. So, what'd your folks do before the Impact?"

Cain answered with a questioning look and silence.

"Hey, we're stuck here together. Might as well get to know each other."

"Dad was a drunk engineer. Mom stayed home and took care of Frank." The last few words tasted bad coming out of his mouth. "What did you do? Before?"

Peters laughed. "A drunk engineer, huh? Sounds like bad combin--"

They were interrupted when the three deadbolts released, and the door eased opened. Cain shot to his feet. Peters sat up on the bed. Cain glanced at him. He seemed calm. Upbeat even.

The barrel of the shotgun poked through the crack. When no one moved, Taggart opened the door and entered, waving the gun back and forth at all of them.

"Peters, give me your hands."

The red-haired man held up his hands, wrists pressed together. His expression didn't change.

"You," Taggart said, pointing at Cain. "Git over 'ere and tie his hands."

Cain tried to catch Frank's eye, but he seemed unconcerned with the old man with a shotgun in the room and was still trying to coax Maisey to the window. This might be their chance, but he wouldn't be able to do it alone. Taggart handed him a ball of twine and motioned him to get busy.

Cain wrapped slow and tried to keep the twine loose without making it obvious. He willed Peters to look at him. Just a quick look would be all that it would take, and they could take Taggart by surprise. Peters seemed to be purposely avoiding eye contact.

"Git to wrappin'!" Taggart yelled and bumped Cain with the stock of the gun.

Cain fumbled the twine and dropped it. The spool ran out a couple of feet before stopping next to Taggart's foot. Peters looked down, and their eyes met for a split second. Cain rolled his eyes toward Taggart. Peters's expression finally changed; he suddenly appeared scared.

Cain bent to pick up the twine, then he reared up, pushing the gun barrel to the right. The gun roared and blasted a hole in the sheetrock wall next to the door. Cain lunged at Taggart's mid-section. Taggart stumbled backward a couple of steps. Peters stood but didn't advance. Maisey barked and growled. Frank realized what was happening and bounded toward his brother. But it was too late. Taggart was able to steady himself on the door and bring the gun to bear on the brothers before they could launch a second attack.

"The hell ya doin'? You stup'd 'r somthin'. I'll shoot ya. Ya ain't wo'th nothin'. Now git 'im tied up 'fore I blow a hole clear through ya."

Cain, still breathing hard, obeyed.

When his wrists were tied, Peters strolled out the door and closed it behind him. One of the deadbolts engaged.

"Shit!" Cain said. "Frank, you gotta pay attention. That was our chance. If you hadn't been messing with that stupid dog..."

"Sorry, Cain," he said and sat down on the floor. He pulled his knees up toward his chest and buried his face in them.

Cain hated when he did that. It was a sure-fire way to bring on the guilt. He wondered if Frank knew it and used it against him, but deep down he knew better. He knew Frank was truly sad that he'd disappointed his little brother, and it was probably tearing him up inside.

"Nah, man, I'm sorry," Cain said, running his fingers through the front of his black hair and pushing it out of his eyes.

* * *

"What's the issue?" The old man asked, keeping the shotgun aimed at his prisoner.

Peters paused for a long time, then smiled. "I've got a deal that will help both of us. You help me clear my name with the Ravens, and I'll give you information that'll make you a rich man."

"I ain't gonna let ya go. Now git back in there."

"You're passing up a big opportunity," Peters said, trying to keep his voice low. "I can give you information that's worth much more than me. But, if you don't want to listen, maybe when the Ravens come to get me, they'll be willing to talk business."

The old bounty hunter lowered his gun. Smoke from his cigarette curled around his thick mustache. He studied the younger man for a long time.

"You let your guard down, old man. I could overpower you before you could get that gun back up to shoot. I could've helped that kid in there, but I didn't. I've had the opportunity to get away twice in the last five minutes."

"Yeah? Then why d'dn't ya?"

"What good would it do me? I'd still be a wanted man. They'd still be chasing me. I don't want to live like a man on the run for the rest of my life. Make this deal to clear my name. You get rich, and I'm a free man again, not constantly watching the shadows behind me. Everybody wins. Well, everybody except those two boys in there."

Taggart seemed to think and let another wave of smoke roll out of his mouth.

"You got somethin' on them?"

Peters grinned. "Sure do."

"They gonna know somethin's up when ya go b'ck in there."

"I got a plan for that too."

* * *

The deadbolt slid again, and Peter's shuffled back into the room. He laid down on the bed and buried his face, letting out a horrible shriek.

"My wife! They killed her! Those sonsabitches killed my wife!"

Chapter 17

The next few days moved in inches. The hot, heavy air made sleep difficult, and the doleful silence grated on Cain's patience. Actually, he didn't know which annoyed him more, the long periods of silence or listening to his brother talk to the dog through the window.

Frank stood at the window for hours petting and talking to her. He seemed to have made progress in gaining her trust. If she was down by the lake, she'd come sauntering up if he called her. Despite Cain's protests, he shared all his food with her. He gave her affection she'd never had before. Sometimes he even fell asleep standing there with his arm stuck out the window petting her.

Part of him was selfishly glad that Frank was focusing on that rather than crying about their mother, but mostly it annoyed him. While Frank's mind seemed to be distracted, Cain's wasn't. He was still bothered by the voice in his head and the memory of his mom's face when the bullets struck her. Her eyes, big and scared. They haunted him. Part of him resented Frank not feeling as burdened by the last few days as he did.

Peters, well, he just didn't like the guy. Every time he spoke, Cain's skin crawled. The guy was way too relaxed. And he didn't seem to have a 'tell.' That made Cain very uncomfortable. He'd dealt with enough shady people in the Crease to know his grandpa was right. Everybody had a tell. Everybody except Peters, apparently. Cain had spent hours thinking back through conversations trying to remember anything that Peters had done that seemed odd. He couldn't think of anything other than his unconcerned attitude. If Peters was truly that confident in his ability to talk his way free, he must have something he could get that the Ravens couldn't get anywhere else.

To top it all off, he still couldn't find a way out. Peters's smug voice echoed in his head: *'If I told ya once, I told ya a million times. There's no way out of here. Might as well relax...'* There was no way he was going to let Peters *'tell'* him anything. He was going to find a way out, but they'd been there four days, and he still hadn't. Acknowledging Peters might be right was not an option. He looked around the room for anything he hadn't tried, but it was the same as it was twenty minutes ago when he did the same exercise.

He was tired of thinking about it.

He went into the bathroom and pulled the hose across the bed, with Peters in it, to Frank standing at the window. Without warning, he ripped off the bandage.

"Ow!" Frank yelled and pulled back.

Maisey jumped to her feet and growled. Her snout poked through the bars and saliva dripped from her mouth.

"Whoa!" Cain said, startled by the sudden ferocity of the dog's reaction.

"Dog's mean. She'll turn on you," Peters said.

"She's not mean. She likes me," Frank replied.

"Remember what happened to the Siegfried and Roy guy? He thought that tiger liked him too. Then she chewed his head off. That dog'll do the same thing to you. Just wait."

Confusion marred Frank's face. "Who?"

"Some guys that used to do a show in Vegas, Frank. Nothing to worry about."

Peters laughed. "Yeah, getting mauled by a wild animal, nothing to worry about."

Cain fumed. The thought of strangling Peters with the hose in his hand flashed through his mind. He pushed it away and looked at Frank's wound. It oozed white liquid, and the red corona had expanded; streaks of red washed all the way across his shoulder and up his neck. The stuff Taggart had given him wasn't enough to kill the infection. Frank needed medical attention.

"Taggart!" Cain yelled out the window.

"What are you calling him for?" Peters said.

"Taggart!"

"He's not going to answer you, fool. Give it up. Let's just sit and talk. Did you play sports in high school?"

"Cain, why are you calling him?" Frank said. That look of fear returned to his face.

"Taggart! You're about to lose your... whatever you thought you could get for Frank! He's gonna lose his arm!"

Frank's face went white. "Cain, am I--"

Cain shook his head very slowly.

"Taggart, he's lying!" Peters yelled. "Don't listen to him!"

Cain pointed at Frank's wound and the bright red streaks emanating from it. "Look at that. He's in serious trouble if we don't get him some real medicine."

He felt Frank tense up.

Maisey growled and scratched her foot in the dirt and dead grass.

Cain glanced her way. Her back arched like an evil black cat on Halloween. Her snarl sent cold ripples running up his back.

"Riiiggghhhtttt. You're like twelve, and you think you're some kind of doctor. Give me a break, kid."

"It doesn't take a freaking doctor to see it's infected and spreading. Taaaaaggart!" Cain turned back to his brother's shoulder, and his stomach churned. The more he looked at it, the more it scared him. "Frank, it'll be okay. But that asshole's not going to pay attention unless he thinks that the money he'll make off you is in jeopardy."

Frank seemed to relax a little; Maisey didn't, though. She paced in a circle growling toward the window.

"I wish I could get some popcorn," Peters said. "This looks promising. Cujo over there is going to make your face look like your shoulder."

"It's okay, girl," Frank said, reaching out for the dog.

"Frank, I need to put some more alcohol on this. It's gonna burn like hell. But, you're gonna have to just grit your teeth and get through it. You gotta be strong, okay? Don't scare your dog. Be strong for her. If she thinks you're scared, she's gonna get scared."

Frank's face fell. "She's not my dog, Cain. She's that guy's dog."

Cain stared hard at his brother. "No, I think she thinks she's your dog," he said, making sure to emphasize the last three words.

Frank's face instantly brightened.

Cain regretted saying it as soon as the words slipped out of his mouth. The last thing they needed if --when-- they got out of here was him wanting to drag 'his' dog along. His ankle had improved over the last few days, but that shoulder was another story. At best, he thought Frank would be severely weakened by the raging infection; he'd already noticed some signs of it over the last couple of days. He had no idea exactly what the worst-case scenario was exactly but assumed the loss of the arm or maybe even death.

At the rate you're going, he's gonna die here, in this room. You keep promising to save him, but you don't deliver. Never deliver. Talk a big game, but when the shit hits the fan, you fail. Just like Gordon. Just like shooting Danny. You weren't even close. Failure!

"I'm okay, girl," Frank said, reaching out and rubbing his fingertips under Maisey's chin.

"On three I'm going to pour. Ready?"

Frank nodded.

"One... two... three."

Cain poured at least a third of the bottle on Frank's wound. He was quiet for a few seconds. Cain ran some cold water from the hose on the infected bite. Frank winced before groaning and trying to escape toward the corner. Cain reached out and hooked his brother around his waist before he could flee.

"Hang in there, Frank."

Maisey snapped her teeth outside the bars.

Cain ignored her and poured a little more alcohol on the wound.

Frank screamed and started to cry. He clutched his arm below his damaged shoulder and pulled away.

The dog barked and pawed at the dirt, reminding Cain of the she-wolf before it attacked.

"Go ahead, get close to that dog now. I dare you."

"Shut up, Peters," Cain snarled.

"It's okay, Maisey. He's trying to help me. It's okay."

"Taggart! We need you!" Cain banged the end of the hose on the window bars.

Finally, they heard footsteps above them and the rattling of empty cans getting kicked out of the way. Taggart stomped down the stairs. Cain counted twelve; there were thirteen steps, so he wasn't coming all the way down. "What," the old man yelled.

Cain tossed the hose, still running, back into the bathroom and talked into the hole in the drywall from the shotgun blast a few days prior. "Taggart, we need a doctor. His shoulder is infected. It's bad. By the time you get someone here to sell him to, he's either going to have one arm or be dead."

"They c'n fix 'im up once they pay fur 'im. Won't be my problem."

"I'm telling you. It will be your problem. Look at it!"

"Christ," Taggart muttered as he stomped down the last step and stalked to the hole in the wall.

Cain motioned for Frank to come over and lower his shoulder so Taggart could see it.

"Yep. It's 'nfected. Don't care. Not my pro'lum."

"What the hell? How's it not your problem?"

"Long's they pay, 'n they'll pay fur a boy that big, promise ya that. Seen it b'fore." Taggart walked away.

Cain counted the thumps Taggart ascended the stairs; each one lit another fire in his gut. The building rage fought with the rising panic inside him, making him a paralyzed bundle of emotion.

For almost a full minute he stood there, wanting. He wanted to die. He wanted to live. He wanted to kill Taggart, Peters. To run as far and as fast as he could, and to just lie down and never wake up.

He slammed his forehead against the wall in the spot that Taggart's face had been peering through. It hurt, but it brought with it some sense of power. Strength. Life. Anger pushed away the good feeling as the thought of Taggart flashed through his consciousness. He smashed his head into the wall again. And again. A tiny piece of the sheetrock gave way. Some dust filtered down across his nose like powdered sugar on a donut.

He wiped it off, looked at the powder on his hand, then at the wall. Excitement rushed through him. He'd found a way out! Now he just needed to find the right time--and hope it wasn't too late to get help for Frank.

Chapter 18

The wind-driven rain drummed against the windows. The constant noise put Garcia's nerves on edge. Doc had limited the amount of pain medicine that he could have. Doc said it was for his protection, but it felt more like spite. Doc was sending a message about who was in charge;

His leg hurt. No, it throbbed, and it was making everything else hurt too. The constant pounding of the rain magnified his discomfort to the point that he wanted to curl up in a ball and scream. Or kill something.

The other truck was fifteen minutes late, and that didn't improve his mood. The plan was simple. Garcia and six men left first to get to the house, bust in, and incapacitate the family; the other truck was to be ten minutes behind. Garcia planned to carry out the interrogation and be back at Nevermore before Doc even noticed he was missing. The delay extended that timeline, putting the whole plan at risk. And kept him away from the pain pills longer.

A middle-aged couple was bound and blindfolded on the floor. The wife screamed for help through choked sobs. Each high-pitched wail caused Garcia to grit his teeth. The husband struggled against his bonds. Garcia nudged him in the ribs with his crutch.

"Stop. Or the next one is going to be with the toe of my boot to the ribs... of your wife. Got it?"

The man stopped struggling. He tried to comfort his wife next to him, but her shrill wails smothered his words.

Headlights flashed across the room. Two doors slammed, and a few seconds later Jovi was led into the house. He was blindfolded and handcuffed. He heard his mom's screams as soon as they got out of the truck and began yelling for her. One of the men flanking him pulled off the blindfold. His eyes fell on his parents tied up on the ground. He burst into tears and tried to lunge for them. The men held him back.

"What are you doing!" he screamed at Garcia.

"We need to talk. Your folks want to make sure you answer honestly."

"I told you everything!"

"Well tell me again because your story is hard to believe."

"Jovi! Jovi!" the woman wailed. She flopped around trying to get free.

"Better tell her to shut the hell up," Garcia said.

"Mom, it's okay. I'm fine. Just relax, and he won't hurt you." He turned to Garcia. "Will you?"

"No promises. Depends on what you tell me."

Jovi's eyes were still full of tears, but he tried to talk them away. "We were tracking them in the woods, and they were hiding behind a pile of dead trees. We didn't see them. The little one fired one shot and got Dylan. I exchanged fire with them. Missed, but they got spooked and fled. Dylan was still alive, so I didn't pursue. I tried to get him out so we could get him help, but I didn't make it."

"Bullshit! Dylan was one of the best soldiers I've ever seen. You expect me to believe that some skinny kid and his oaf brother got the drop on him. No way." Garcia nodded to one of the men who pressed a gun to the back of the dad's head.

"It's what happened! Don't hurt him. Please!"

The mom kicked her feet and screamed. Garcia closed his eyes and breathed. Red flashes burst behind his eyelids in time with his pulse. His leg hurt so bad the nerves in his teeth tingled.

"I still don't believe you. If what you're saying is true, they had numbers and were hidden where they could snipe from, why'd they let you live? Why not just keep firing until they took you out too? It's what I would do."

Jovi shrugged. "The kid didn't seem like the type that wanted to kill anybody."

"What do you mean by that," Garcia asked, raising his eyebrow.

"He could've killed me. In fact, he said as much,"

Both parents started kicking and yelling.

Garcia took a deep breath to try to numb the pulsing ache. It didn't work. Every fiber in his body pulsed with the pain. The wind blasted another burst of rain against the window, causing Garcia to wince at the sudden noise. He propped himself on his crutch and swung his foot. His boot struck the dad in the ribs. The man's face contorted as he writhed on the floor.

"Enough!" Garcia said and then hobbled close to where his men held Jovi. "So, you had a conversation with the kid while Dylan was bleeding out?" His voice got shriller with each word.

"Not really a conversation. He was hidden, and I was trying to take cover after Dylan went down. He called out to me. Told me he could've already killed me. Tried to talk me into running. Said the resistance could protect me."

Rage at what he was hearing erupted inside Garcia. He lunged forward, ignoring the objections from his leg. It was in a cast, but pressure still sent bolts of pain through him. The rage was strong enough to harness the pain and turn it outward. Emptying all the pain and anger into one swing, he punched Jovi right under the ribcage.

Jovi gasped for air and doubled over. His mom shrieked, and his dad bashed the back of his head against the gun. The Raven pushed him back down, put a knee in the middle of his back, and pressed the gun hard against his head.

Garcia bent over and whispered in Jovi's ear. "You should've run. You kill mine, I kill yours. That's what Poe says, right?"

Garcia forced Jovi's head up. The kid was still squeaking when he tried to breathe, and tears poured down his cheeks. "No," he tried to say, but it was little more than a desperate wheeze.

"Do it," Garcia ordered.

The Raven's face went white. "You... we... you can't just kill the guy."

"Do it. That's an order."

Garcia felt the pressure building again. The pulsing pain. The wind and rain beating against the windows. The anger at that snot-faced little probie. They all amplified each other until he felt like screaming, beating, murdering. Anything to unload some tension.

"You're crazy. I'm not shooting a defenseless man." He lowered the gun. "You said that we were just gonna shake up the probie a little. This is too--"

Before he could finish, Garcia was on top of him and had ripped the gun away. He tried to push himself free, but Garcia had managed to flip the gun around and pistol-whipped him with it. The younger guy fell back, but Garcia followed, hitting him a second and a third time.

Garcia pushed himself to his feet. His blonde hair had slipped out of its tie and hung wild around his face. He winced as the subsiding anger let the pain sink in. One look at Jovi and the sight of the insubordinate punk once again primed his temper.

He fired twice at Jovi's dad.

"DDDDDaaaaaaaddddddd!"

Headlights splayed across the wall again and stayed on.

He fired three times at Jovi's mom.

Jovi tugged himself free and raced toward Garcia; tears and splatters of blood wetted his face. He tackled Garcia around the waist and drove him against the wall. Jovi stomped down on the cast. Garcia howled and dropped the gun. Jovi kicked his cast, then landed a punch above his eye, splitting his brow open.

A pair of muscular arms wrapped around Jovi's chest and pulled him away. Garcia slid down the wall.

Doc charged through the door, trailed by six men with assault rifles. They spread out around the room, weapons aimed at Garcia's men. Doc eyes darted around the room, and his face turned bright red. He rushed to Garcia and pulled him to his feet.

"What the hell did you do?" he demanded and shoved Garcia hard against the wall. "What the hell? You stupid son--" He threw Garcia to the ground and turned to one of his men. "Handcuff him and get him out of here."

Jovi jerked free and lunged at Garcia again, landing two more punches to the face before getting pulled back.

Doc rushed over, examined the parents, and shook his head. He moved to Jovi and put his hand on the boy's shoulder.

"I'm sorry."

"Sorry?! You're sorry?!" Jovi's face was contorted with rage and sorrow. The headlights shining in the window shimmered in the tears on his cheeks.

Doc looked at the ground and paused until Garcia had been escorted out into the storm.

"You have a sister, right?"

Fear flashed across Jovi's face. He didn't speak.

"Do you know where she is? We'll keep her safe. You have my word."

"I don't know. And I don't trust you," Jovi said.

Doc ran his fingers through his salt and pepper hair, then addressed one of his men. "Get him back to Nevermore. Take all weapons away from him and put him in an officer's room. I'll figure something out when I get back."

"I'm not leaving!" Jovi jerked and struggled to break free from the hands gripping him.

Yes, you are. Take him. Now!" Doc said.

Chapter 19

Gabriel wandered through the sanctuary of his church, running his fingers over the backs of the pews as he walked. He loved the way the sun used the stained glass to cast a beautiful array of colors on the floor. It reminded him that there was still good in the world. It gave him hope, and hope was something that seemed in short supply these days. Today, though, it didn't give him the same uplifting feeling that it normally did.

Just an hour ago, he'd stood at the altar and gazed out at the faithful and wondered if he was offering them any hope. The loss of David and Beth Benoit loomed over the congregation like a menacing specter. Their murder, without evidence, without a trial, based solely on the whim of one man, had a noticeable effect on everyone gathered. Their prayers were quieter, and they made less eye contact with him. Instead, they looked around the church, as if wondering who would be dead next.

During his sermon, he compared the oppression of the Ravens to the Egyptians that enslaved the Israelites. But God sent Moses to defeat the Egyptians and lead His chosen people to the promised land. Gabriel promised his congregation that God would send them a new

Moses to defeat the Ravens and lead them out of oppression.

The problem was that the one he believed to be the new Moses hadn't been heard from in a week. Considering the size of the bounty on him, he was probably dead. Even if his new Moses wasn't dead, he didn't know if there was anywhere out there for him to lead the people to. He was fairly sure there was no land flowing with milk and honey out there. Only lands flowing with radiation and death.

Gabriel hoped his voice and face didn't belie his doubts to the congregation. He told himself that it was for their own good. The world was a dismal place without hope. His job was to make sure they held onto it, even if it meant not being honest about his personal feelings.

He'd spent his entire adult life not being honest about how he felt; he should have been quite adept at it. But despite the fact he'd spent twenty years leading a double life without anyone finding out about Emily or their daughter, Maggie, he still felt like his guilt betrayed him at every turn.

He was startled from his thoughts by the silhouette of a thin, leggy woman leaning in the doorway to the vestibule. The bright sunlight behind her gave her an other-worldly glow. She stood and strolled toward him, her heels clicking on the marble floor.

"Father, I need to confess," she said. "I'm sorry--"

Gabriel shook his head. "Don't call me father. I'm not a priest anymore, Angel."

"Well, Gabriel, I want you to know I'm sorry about the other day. And the fact that you have fifty or sixty people show up every few days to hear you preach means that you are still a priest. You shouldn't beat yourself up over a... an indiscretion. Forgive yourself. Plus, who knows if Rome even exists anymore. You might be the Pope as far as you know."

"Emily wasn't just an indiscretion. That was a decision to turn from God's will. And a decision that I can't be forgiven for because I'm not sorry."

Gabriel hated the words as they came out of his mouth. He wanted to be sorry, to ask God to forgive him. Breaking a vow isn't just a little white lie. He didn't just break his vow, he broke it repeatedly for twenty years. And he knew he was now teetering on the brink of doubling down.

She put her forearm on his shoulder and ran her fingers through the back of his thick gray hair. He pulled away, then moved back toward her. He closed his eyes and absorbed the warmth of her touch.

"Any contact with Maggie?" he asked.

She shook her head and frowned. "The crickets have been chirping loud, but nothing about Maggie. Lots of talk about the boy. He's alive."

Gabriel felt his spirits sink, but they were buoyed a little by the news that Cain was alive. He felt hope gaining strength in him but pushed it back down for fear of the 'but' that was sure to follow.

"The Ravens are in an uproar about it," she continued. "Apparently he beat the crap out of Poe--who's in critical condition. And there's more. Apparently, Garcia, the really built blonde guy, is Poe's son and he didn't want that information out."

Gabriel pulled back again. The hope that was springing inside him faded, replaced by guilt.

"Don't do that," she said.

"Do what?"

"This situation is not at all similar to yours. And you're getting' all angsty about it. You didn't tell Maggie the truth to protect her."

"Did I? Or did I do it because it was easier to try to pretend I wasn't living a lie if I was just 'Uncle Gabe?' I can't even answer that question myself."

"You were part of her life. A big part. It wasn't like you just disappeared on her and her mom. You helped raise her. You supported her. You hugged her when she hurt and celebrated with her when she was proud. I wish I could've had someone like that in my life. Even if--" She stopped talking and turned her head.

Gabriel reached out and pulled her to him. He felt her body shiver with silent tears. He held her for over a minute and let her cry. Then he released her, stepped back, and tilted her head up so he could see her eyes. So beautiful and dark, like windows to a wounded soul. He marveled at how well she hid her scars and wondered if any other person in the world knew the depth of her pain. He suspected not. The version of her that she showed the world was strong and seductive; the version he knew was vulnerable and scared. That worried him that she let him get that close. He didn't want her to love him, but he knew she did.

And he didn't want to love her but knew he did.

"How do you know this? About Poe and the kid?" he said, trying to bring the conversation back around to something less intimate.

She choked out a tear-interrupted laugh. "Never ask a woman about her sources," she said, wiping her eyes and forcing a smile. "I told you the crickets have been chirping loud the last few days."

"So, do your crickets know where the boy is?"

Her face fell again. "No. He disappeared. No one's heard from him since Poe raided his house."

Gabriel felt his hope follow Angel's face. If no one had heard from him, that likely meant that either they found him and killed him or found him and were holding him captive. Either option was bad.

"I see your gears turning... and forget it. He's alive. They wouldn't be freaking out like they are if they had any reason to believe he's dead. They're in full-blown panic mode. They believe he's alive, so I believe he's alive."

"You believe--"

"I believe in you. You. Father Gabriel Farr." Her fingers slid through the back of his hair. "I forget that sometimes. If you trust this kid, then I need to, too."

Gabriel smiled and leaned into her. He closed his eyes as her fingers caressed his scalp.

"The crickets are also saying that you sent a squad out to try to save the kid and his family, but they were pretty much vaporized because the Ravens have a .50 caliber gun mounted on a truck," she said.

"I did. And, yes, it went poorly. They were headed to the boy's home and heard gunshots. Bingham split the group. Three went to the home, three to investigate the shots. They engaged forces in a Raven truck that looked stalled on the side of the road. They were advancing on it when the Ravens rolled up with the big gun and unleashed it on them. They didn't have much of a chance."

"I might have a solution. A guy approached me in the Crease the other day," Angel said, lowering her voice to not much more than a whisper even though they were alone in the church. "He says he can get his hands on an RPG that can take out that truck. Military grade stuff."

Gabriel raised his eyebrows and pulled back so he could look at her. "Really? What's he want?"

"Didn't pursue it that far yet. Wasn't sure if you'd be interested or if you were thinking that we needed to back off a little. The casualty list is getting too long."

Gabriel sighed. He didn't need reminding that he had blood on his hands. The casualty list had grown substantially in the last week, at least three on his orders. The Ravens were getting more aggressive--and brutal. Maybe blowing that weapon to smithereens would put a little hesitation in their minds.

"I'm willing to talk," he said. "Set it up."

Chapter 20

Doc found Poe in the massive greenhouse behind Nevermore, exactly where he expected to find him. Poe always said he could think better there because gardening was his way of working off stress in the old days. He liked getting his hands dirty. Their prepper group even had a community garden on one of the back acres of his ranch. The two men had spent many evenings swapping stories, sharing beers, and pulling weeds with their friends. Now, there were people to do it all for them, but Doc knew that when something was troubling his friend, that would be the place he retreated to.

"How you feeling, buddy?" Doc said, gently touching Poe's back.

Poe turned and looked up from the wheelchair he was sitting in. Both eyes were still a muted red where blood mingled with the acid damage. The area around them was a sickly shade of green and purple punctuated by several black stitches above the right. He winced when he turned and moved his cracked rib.

"How do I look," he said, faking a smile that revealed a mouthful of broken and missing teeth.

"Honestly? Like shit. But you're alive. You're lucky."

Poe pursed his lips and turned back to a bean plant. He ran his fingers up the stalk. "Plants are so much easier than people. You take care of them. They appreciate it and provide you with food. People, not so much. They'll turn on you."

"Dogs might be a more appropriate analogy. You take care of them, and they love you, and they'll fight to protect you. They don't look at two people decide which one will treat them better. But people do. If they have a reason to believe someone else might offer something better, they'll change their loyalty. Hope for something better changes everything, especially if one option is pain or suffering. They'll choose the second option on just hope alone."

Poe rolled a few feet away and examined another plant, seemingly oblivious to Doc's words.

"The Skinny Cain kid. He's Allen's kid. I knew as soon as I saw him," Poe said.

"Well, you probably knew as soon as you heard the name, didn't you?"

"Yeah. I guess. I was just hoping that it wasn't the case. Found out that Allen's dead. Wife and both boys were still living out there," Poe closed his eyes, leaned back in his chair, and took a long breath. "I ordered Danny and Garcia to leave all their guns. We were going to see an old friend. I didn't want guns. I thought we'd ride out there. I'd sit down, maybe have a drink with Allen, and fill him in on what his kid was doing. Remind him of the deal we made and that he needed to reign in the boy before I revoked my side of the deal."

"Damn. So, did the wife or kids even know about the deal? I know he wasn't telling her what we were doing back in those early days. Didn't want to freak her out. Hell, he wouldn't even bring her around us before Impact. It's possible she didn't have any idea that he was one of us."

Poe drew in a long breath and winced. "I guess it's possible. But can you really keep that kind of stuff from your wife? I mean wouldn't he have to tell her why the boys weren't going for evaluations at seventeen like every other boy?"

Doc leaned against a shelf of plants. He remembered when Allen wanted to leave. Poe was devastated. The three of them had worked together for years before the Impact to make sure that if something ever happened, they'd be in a position to grab power and influence. They planned to be able to provide for people and earn their loyalty, and it worked perfectly until the farms came into the picture. Allen always vehemently opposed doing business with the farms, and the thought of his oldest son being sent there wasn't something he thought he could do. He told Poe he wanted out. Said that he would keep to himself outside of town and not oppose anything the Ravens did if Poe would forget his boys existed when they turned seventeen. The next four or five days, Poe wandered around in the greenhouses and refused to see anyone before he finally agreed to the deal. But something changed in him during those days. He came out the other side more decisive but more fearful of losing what they'd built. And much quicker to anger.

"When'd he die? Maybe he died before the kids turned seventeen. The way he talked about his wife, she didn't sound like the rebel type. Especially if it meant her kids would be in danger."

Poe leveled his gaze at his old friend and tried to shrug, but cut it short as the look of pain rocked his face.

"Can't you do anything for these ribs?"

Doc shook his head. "Just pain meds and afraid to give you too many of those because I don't want them fogging your brain. You need to be able to think clearly."

Poe sighed.

"Some of it we can talk about later. But there are some things we have to come up with a plan for."

Poe motioned for Doc to continue.

"Your son. Your secret is out. And he's out of control."

Doc went on to tell Poe what had happened during the escape from the Coldrake house culminating in McCoy telling everyone he could about Garcia's lineage. Each sentence seemed to stoke Poe's frustration. He pushed himself to his feet and swept a bunch of plants onto the floor, their ceramic pots shattering in a chorus of cracks. Poe gritted his broken teeth at the sudden movement of his ribcage.

"You should sit down for the rest of this," Doc said, trying to guide his friend back to the wheelchair.

"There's more?"

Doc nodded. Poe banged his fist on the shelf that he'd just emptied.

"The probie that went into the woods with Dylan. Garcia didn't believe his version of the story. So, he took his unit and Dylan's unit to the kid's house and murdered his parents right in front of him."

Poe was silent and lowered himself into the chair.

"Remember what I was saying about how people will blindly choose other option if it the original option might hurt them? We're losing our grip, Boss. You hanging people in the street, everyone finding out you were hiding the fact that Garcia is your son, and now he's murdering people with their hands and feet tied. Not to mention the horror stories coming out of the farms. It's bad. We're losing control because we offer hurt, suffering, death, and this resistance group is offering hope. The rumors from down around Cowley and Dennison are that you and Garcia are hunting down anyone that utters a word wrong. Men down there reported intercepting resistance propaganda yesterday. People think the unknown might be better than what they have."

"We'll send every man we have to search until we catch Skinny Cain. We'll make an example out of him. Then we'll go after the resistance and make examples out of them one by one until they lose the will to fight."

"Are you listening to me?" Doc said, his voice getting higher with each word. "People aren't dogs that you can beat into submission! The more brutal you are, the more power you give to the resistance. The more their hope seems appealing."

Poe's eyes narrowed. "Whose side are you on?"

Doc recoiled a little. He knew Poe was lashing out because he didn't like what he was hearing, but it didn't make those words hurt less.

"I'm on the side of what we set out to build. Civilization. And I don't want to see that jeopardized because you and your son suddenly decide that murdering people will keep them in line. The last thing you want to do is give them a face to rally behind."

"Every civilization throughout history has had steep punishments for disloyalty!"

"And what happened to all those civilizations? You see any of them around? I don't."

The doors are the far end of the greenhouse swung open.

"Sorry to interrupt, sir," an older soldier said.

Doc recognized him as Thomas 'Sly' Sylvester. He volunteered early on and had been moving up the ranks ever since. The structure and purpose suited him, but these were the kind of guys that would be fighting for the resistance if he couldn't get Poe to recognize where they'd gone off the tracks.

"What is it?" Poe asked, the impatience clear in his voice.

The soldier stepped in and closed the door behind him. "It seems the Skinny Cain boy has been captured," he said.

Doc and Poe both stood up and stared at the soldier.

"A bounty hunter on the Chixaposse arm of the lake claims to have captured him and the older brother and is holding them. He also claims to have another man that killed two of our men."

Poe looked at Doc and smiled. "Good things come to those who wait."

"Is there anything else?"

"Yes. The Usher Outpost reports having caught two men that were trying to break in. Both of the men have been reported missing from Farm 1256."

Doc sighed and rubbed his temples. "That it?"

"Yessir."

"Thanks, Sly," Doc said.

"Lieutenant, send word to the bounty hunter that I will personally come to pick up the captives the day after tomorrow. I'll need a boat prepped and two capos. And a driver, too."

"Do you want Garcia as one of the capos, sir. He's being held--"

"No, not Garcia. Doc will advise you which men. But this time we're going with guns. Fool me once shame on you, fool me twice shame on me." Poe paused, then looked at Doc. "How many men do we have at Usher?"

"Usually four. Sometimes as many as six. But we're spread pretty thin."

"We're going to keep the prisoners there until I'm ready for their executions. Make sure we send all of Dylan's crew out there."

"Can't do it," Doc said. "This place is easier to defend. Why don't you bring them here?"

"Because if by chance this 'resistance' grabs their pitchforks and storms the Bastille to rescue them, they won't be here. Even if they just--"

"They've got more than just pitchforks. And they're much more likely to do a frontal assault on a little outpost than they are here."

Poe shook his head. "Not if they don't know the prisoners are out there."

"Fine. Send Scarlett out there too. Even if it's sparsely defended, that gun in that truck made mincemeat out of a couple of 'em. They'll think twice about attacking it."

"How many technicals do we have right now?"

"One with a .50 caliber M2. Two more with M60s. Working on a deal for two more fifties, but haven't finalized it yet," Doc answered.

Poe nodded. "Okay send the big gun."

The soldier smirked. "Yessir."

"Dismissed, Sly. And.. thank you," Doc said. He waited until after the soldier had left and closed the door before he spoke. "Harry, I don't--"

"The name's Poe now. Harry died."

Doc put his hand on Poe's shoulder. "Harry isn't dead. Harry is my oldest friend, and I'm looking right at him. It's Harry I'm talking to, not Poe. I think my friend has let his other persona go too far and lost himself. This resistance is small, but it can grow if Poe keeps pushing."

Poe lowered his head for a minute then raised it to meet his friend's eyes. "As your friend, I'll say that we'll talk more about it later. But our priority is crushing the will of this resistance. As your boss, I'll say to meet me at the market at noon the day after tomorrow. End of discussion."

With that, Poe turned and walked slowly toward the door.

Chapter 21

Cain had been standing at the window for three hours waiting to see Taggart trudge down the hill to the water. He watched a storm billow up, blow through, and then return to the oppressive sun cooking the ground. The fishing boat bobbed in its slip as the wind blew a few little waves across the water. It floated empty and unused.

"Why the hell isn't he going fishing. He's gone every day since we got here," Cain said.

"Why do you care?" Peters said.

Cain ignored him and looked over at his brother who, as usual, stood with his arm out the window. He stroked Maisey's back, and she curled up pressed as close as she could get to the window. The last two days when Taggart had trudged down to the dock and called for her, she stayed by the window with Frank. That dog and come to love Frank as much as he loved her.

Cain smiled. For the first time in a week, maybe longer, it was a genuine smile. He'd always known he'd have to take care of Frank forever, and he'd always resented it. But now, he felt a closeness and affection for his brother that he couldn't remember ever feeling. The feeling brought with it a contentment and hope that he hadn't known since before the Impact.

"Frank, when we get out of here, we'll get you a dog."

Frank, it's my fault your momma is dead, but I'll get you a dog instead. Nice trade.

"I want Maisey. I can't leave her here. He'll be mean to her."

"Okay, we'll try to take Maisey."

You will not. Why lie to him? You'll probably kill the dog too.

Footsteps thudded around above their heads. A door slammed. Taggart clomped down the concrete stairs and the hill toward the dock.

"Maisey! Let's go ya l'zy bitch," he yelled without turning around.

"It's okay, girl. You don't have to go. Cain's gonna get us outta here and then you can come live with us," Frank whispered.

"You dumbass, Cain ain't going anywhere, and neither are you or that flea-bag dog."

Cain watched until Taggart had started the engine, backed out of the slip, and raced down the cove.

"You're wrong, Peters. We're getting out of here now," Cain said. "Frank, come here. We're gonna knock all this sheetrock out under this hole." He started banging the palm of his hand under the hole the shotgun had made. After four or five hits, a piece chunked off.

"No way is Frankenstein getting out through there. The other side is two-by-six studs on sixteen-inch centers. I wouldn't even fit, and I'm a lot smaller than he is."

Cain turned to Peters. His eyes glimmered. "No, he won't fit. But I will. And I can unlock the door from the other side."

When the shit hits the fan, you'll run and leave them both here. Just like you did with Gordon. Just watched them take him away. Did nothing.

Frank rushed to the hole and started throwing his good shoulder against the hole. After a couple of lunges, a foot-and-a-half long piece broke off and fell to the ground.

"That's it, Frank. Just hit it a few times to crack it, then we can pull or push on it to get it to break off."

Peters sat up in bed. "No! What are you thinking? Even if you get out, you've still got a price on your heads. You're still gonna live your life looking over your shoulder, waiting for the next bounty hunter to grab you. Hell no!"

What he said didn't even register with Cain, who focused on breaking off another six-inch chunk of wall.

"If you stay here, you're for sure gonna die!" Cain yelled. "Now get over here and help us."

Peters climbed off the bed and forced his way in front of the hole, blocking it. "No. You aren't doing this."

"The hell we aren't! Get out of the way!"

Frank grabbed Peters by the arm and tried to pull him away.

"You better back off, kid," Peters seethed.

Frank moved closer, grabbing Peters by the neck. Peters stomped hard on Frank's bad ankle. Frank wailed in pain and released his hold. Peters lunged at Frank's chest sending them stumbling backward until they collapsed on the bed.

Maisey launched to her feet. She growled and snarled. Her snout stuck through the bars, and her teeth clicked together. Peters pushed on Frank's throat.

"I'm not gonna let you screw this up for me! I'm not gonna spend the rest of my life looking over my shoulder!"

Cain launched himself at Peters, pushing him off of Frank, and knocking him to the floor. Cain paused when Peters's words sunk in. Hatred swept over him like an ocean wave. Maisey's teeth snapped at the air, her unrelenting eyes trained on Peters who writhed on the floor holding his ribs. In that moment, Cain wished he could help her through the window.

"You sold us out, didn't you? Didn't you! That's why you've been so confident you can make a deal. We're your chips!" Cain screamed. How could he be so stupid? He searched his memory for anything he'd said to tip Peters off. Nothing came to him. "That wasn't a letter to your wife, was it? You used it to tell the old man who we were, didn't you? You son of a bitch!"

"Skinny Cain! As soon as you said your name was Cain and you hung out in the Crease, I knew exactly who you were. I knew you scavenged weapons for the resistance. I knew you helped that ex-priest smuggle seventeen-year-olds out of Raven territory. Not a lot of scrawny kids named Cain that are known in the Crease."

Cain cringed. How could he be so stupid? So arrogant. He doubted Peters's story that he had connections in the Crease. Now his arrogance stung him.

Frank charged forward and slammed his entire bulk into the wall. He howled in pain. A foot-sized piece bowed out. Frank backed up for another run. He charged again. After he hit the wall, he turned his head upward and roared in agony.

Maisey barked and growled. Cain clawed at the weakened sheetrock.

Frank limped back to take a fourth run, holding his good shoulder.

"Hang in there, Frank. We're getting the hell outta here. Then we'll get you all fixed up, so you don't hurt anymore, okay?"

Frank nodded and readied himself for the next charge. Maisey's growls alerted him to the danger, but it was too late. The garden hose struck him hard across the face. The metal coupling split the skin below his eyebrow, splattering blood in a line of red dots across the faded blue wall. Frank was still reeling from the first blow when Peters swung the hose again, striking his wounded shoulder and tearing the bandage loose. Frank screamed and clutched his arm, dropping to his knees. Three rivers of blood marked his face like stripes on a vertically hanging flag.

Peters pulled the hose back to take another swing. Cain lunged at his legs, wrapping them and causing him to lose his balance. Peters stumbled backward, eventually falling against the wall.

A two-foot section fell away.

Frank, still holding his arm, got to his feet and lunged at Peters. He landed, wounded shoulder first, under Peters's ribcage. Peters gasped as the air rushed out of his lungs. He squatted, one hand braced against his knee for support, the other clutched his chest in a desperate attempt to breathe.

Maisey backed up and pushed forward, trying to force as much of her head between the bars as she could get. She snapped her jaws and snarled at Peters.

Cain scrambled to his feet and charged again. He drove his shoulder into Peters's head. The red-headed man's nose erupted blood as it broke; his head slammed hard against the wall. Sheetrock cracked. Peters slumped to the floor in a crimson heap. Cain pushed him aside.

"Frank, it's gonna give. Another couple times and it'll be big enough for me to fit through!"

The older brother made another run, slamming himself into the wall and howling in pain.

A piece broke free. Cain kicked at it. Another six inches and he'd be able to squeeze through.

In the commotion neither of them noticed the fishing boat's outboard motor returning.

Frank hobbled at the wall and slammed against it again. Another chunk of sheetrock cracked and fell away. Cain slipped through the hole.

He flipped the knobs on the three deadbolts and swung the door open.

"Frank, let's go!"

Maisey yelped and raised up on her hind legs, the barrel of a pistol poised under her chin.

"No poin' in dat, boys. See, I'll kill this damn dog as quick as I'd kill you. Quicker prolly. She ain't good fer nothin'."

Frank collapsed to the floor. "Don't hurt her. I'll stay. I'll stay."

Chapter 22

Gabriel descended the steps into the black-market area of the Crease. He gave his ticket to the guard and didn't pretend he didn't know where to go. At this point, he felt like he was on a mission from God, pretending that he didn't belong wasn't needed anymore. He was a soldier on the side of God against the forces of evil. A man of God goes into the lion's den if it's the right thing to do.

He paused outside the doorway to the market area and said a prayer for continued guidance.

At this moment, his past didn't matter. The fact that he was in love with another woman didn't matter. Nothing mattered except saving thousands of people from Raven brutality. And he believed the way to do that was through that door. He took a deep breath and walked through it, immediately looking for Angel.

It didn't take him long to spot her walking toward him, her white gossamer gown and dirty white wings flowing behind her. A nervous-looking man followed on her heels. Puffy dark-black circles trembled as his eyes darted toward every shadowed nook and cranny in the place. He tugged at his jacket and straightened his tie. Despite the clothes, the guy had the gravitas of a sixteen-year-old boy on his first date in a car.

As they approached, Angel smiled. She reached out and put her hands in the back of his thick gray hair. The nervous guy stood there like the sixteen-year-old boy whose first date just went off to dance with a football player.

"Hey, darlin'. You lookin' for a threesome?" she said, her voice deeper and more sultry than it naturally was.

Her perfume hit him. They'd never slept together, but that perfumed oozed sex. He closed his eyes, breathed it in, and again prayed for strength.

"Sure. If the price is right," he said.

Angel smiled. "Follow us. I'll make it worth your while. We can talk price later." She winked.

Gabriel followed them to Angel's room. She lit two candles. Her perfume filled the whole room. He shut his eyes and imagined what it would be like to make love to her. Then he shook himself. He had a job to do, and he needed to focus on that.

"Father Farr, this is Mongoose. Mongoose, this is Father Farr."

Gabriel held out his hand; Mongoose took it, but without much of a grip.

"First time selling contraband weapons, eh?" Gabriel said, motioning for Mongoose to have a seat at the table.

"No. I've sold a lot of weapons. Come across them all the time," Mongoose said. His eyes roamed around the room as he pulled out one of the wooden chairs and sat down. Gabriel pulled out the other one, spun it around, and sat backward on it, resting his arms on the curved top rail.

"Let's be real. You come across handguns, maybe the occasional semi-automatic. Those are a dime a dozen in here. This is your first time dealing with something that'll get you killed if you make a deal with the wrong person. Am I right?"

Mongoose nodded.

"Thought so. Well, you came to the right place. I'll do you right."

"Good," he said. "I don't want to go to the Ravens with it, but I will if I have to."

Gabriel shook his head. "No, you won't. If you had loyalty to them, they'd have been your first stop. Without a doubt, their budget is bigger than mine. You came here because you don't want them to have it."

The man's eyes doubled in size, apparently surprised that Gabriel could read him that well. Gabriel wasn't sure how he felt about this guy. It was good that he wasn't some big-time arms dealer that would sell his mother for the right price, but he also didn't have much of a poker face if he got pinched by the Ravens later.

"So, what exactly do you have?"

"I have an RPG-7 launcher and two HEAT warheads."

"Only two? Doesn't give us much room for error. Aren't those things notoriously hard to aim?"

"Actually, at a hundred yards or less, they are deadly accurate, even in a strong wind. Beyond a hundred yards the accuracy drops off significantly."

When Mongoose talked about the weapon, his voice was deep and firm, and his eyes could bore holes through rock. It was the rest of the time that made Gabriel nervous. The guy was jittery, and his eyes never quit moving. The look on Angel's face made Gabriel think she had noticed the difference, too.

"U.S. made or Soviet?" Gabriel asked.

"Soviet."

"Where does a guy in the middle of the United States happen upon a Soviet rocket launcher?"

"Never said that I found it around here," Mongoose said, his voice still firm and confident. "There are survivors outside of Raven territory that are willing to make deals. Leave it at that."

"Then why did you risk bringing into Raven territory? Why not deal it somewhere else?"

Mongoose sat silently. His eyes darted around the room like he was following a fly

Gabriel watched him for about ten seconds before he said, "Because you're actually from here and you hate the Ravens. It's worth a little extra risk to see it inflict some damage to them."

"Yeah. Pretty much." His voice wasn't as confident anymore. "Lots of other places have their own versions of the Ravens. I'd rather it get used on the devil I know rather than the devil I don't."

Gabriel smiled. "Now you're talking my language." He paused and then said, "I'll give you a full pig. You can have her alive or butchered, your call."

Mongoose looked like he was thinking.

"You should take it. It's a good deal, and you've already said you want to see it used against the Ravens," Angel said.

Mongoose nodded. "Deal," he said.

After a few minutes of finalizing details of the switch, Mongoose left.

Angel smiled and sauntered toward Gabriel. He stood and pulled her into an embrace. He didn't want to let her go, but eventually, he did. He pulled a radio out of the back of his jeans.

"It's a go," he said. "Get me someone watching Nevermore. I want to know as soon as that beast rolls out of there. We're gonna blow that mother effer sky high."

Chapter 23

Poe winced and sucked in a long breath as Doc slid the needle between his ribs.

"That's the first one. You sure you want the second?" Doc asked.

Poe nodded without taking another breath, and Doc repeated the procedure. Poe yelled and banged his fist on the hospital bed.

"You'll feel some relief in about thirty minutes. But, as your doctor, I need to advise you against doing too much. Those are strong pain meds. I'd also recommend against going after those kids today. Bounty hunter has them. They're safe there for another day or two."

Poe allowed himself to be pulled up to a seated position. "As your patient, I understand the risks, but this has to happen today. All of it. As painful as it's gonna be. As long as you've made sure that everything is set up like I detailed, I'll be fine."

"What if that bounty hunter sold you out to the resistance, and they're waiting for you? You'd be a lot easier to protect in a caravan along the road." Doc slid the curtain open.

"By boat, it's fifteen or twenty minutes. Four times that by road. And let's face it, the water will be a smoother ride,"--he motioned to his padded ribs--"not like there's any boat traffic stirring up waves out there. You said I'm still gonna feel anything that jolts me, didn't you? Kinda want to avoid that as much as possible."

Doc furrowed his brow. "Why don't you let me go instead. I'll get them--"

"Oh hell naw," Poe said, something that resembled half of a smile inching across his face. "They're mine. Besides, you're gonna be busy here. You've got me two good men for security, and extra guns in the boat, right?"

Doc nodded. "Got a driver, too. That Jovi Fields kid, the one that Garcia *murdered* his parents, volunteered. I told him he could take time off to get his head right, but he wants to go. Blames the brothers for his folks' deaths. He grew up on the lake and apparently used to race boats, so he's an experienced captain. You okay with that?"

Poe nodded. "Yeah, if he's got a vendetta, he's a guy I want with me." He took a deep breath, stood, and walked toward the door, frowning. "Meet me in the middle of Main Street in an hour. And have your medical crap with you."

Chapter 24

Gabriel tried to steady his arms on the roof of the truck cab as it bounced along the dilapidated road. He peered through binoculars but still couldn't find it. The truck, its big gun manned and protected by at least three other soldiers, had rolled out of Nevermore about twenty minutes ago headed this direction; Gabriel's vehicle followed it, about ten minutes behind. He was glad that it was headed this way because it didn't have many intersecting roads and there wasn't much out this way except for a Raven storehouse.

"You see anything?" he said, holding the binoculars out to the man next to him. Billy Gentry stood just a little under six-feet tall and was almost as wide. All muscle. He wore a tight beige shirt with an upside-down American flag, and his camouflage pants looked like his thighs were about to bust out of them. Before the Impact, he had spent twelve years in the Army and another eight in the Reserves. Now, he was on the downhill side of forty but was still an expert marksman. Since they only had two shots at destroying this thing, Gabriel didn't know of anyone better to take them.

Billy took the binoculars and looked through them.

"Nah. Oh, hold on--"

"We're catching up with them," the driver yelled back to the older men. "You can see where the dust is rising from their tires up ahead."

Gabriel looked and saw it. He spun his head around to look behind them. The same dust cloud. Cold fear ripped his breath away.

"Get off the road. Now!"

It was too late.

He heard the repeated THUNK of the gun at the same time the windshield and back window exploded, painting the truck bed with a sickening wash of red.

The horn blared a monotone death knell.

Billy jumped over the side. Gabriel tossed the pack carrying the launcher and rockets to him; he went to slip over the side but felt something warm and wet on his leg. He looked down and saw it was his blood. A piece of glass had sliced into his thigh.

The cannon on the other truck roared three more times, jolting his truck as the rounds ripped apart the engine.

"I'm hit!" he yelled.

Billy rushed around to the back and lowered the tailgate. He climbed up into the bed and examined the wound. "Yeah, it's deep but missed anything major. God was lookin' out for ya, Padre." He peeked up and saw the dust cloud rising again. "They're coming this way. Grab the pack. I'm gonna throw you over my shoulders."

Billy pushed Gabriel to the edge and pulled him up over his shoulders in a fireman's carry. "Been a long time since I did this," he grunted as he took his first tentative step. When his legs held, he took the second.

The tires on the road were getting louder.

Billy picked up the pace and before long was in a light jog across the uneven ground. He stumbled once but recovered his balance.

Gabriel looked back. They'd move deep enough into the thick trees that he couldn't see any part of their truck or the gunship. He heard voices over the blaring horn, but they didn't seem to be coming any closer.

Billy slowed. He bent over and lowered Gabriel to the ground.

"We're gonna need to get you stitched up," Billy said, taking off his belt. He dug through the pack and found an old Ace bandage. Not gonna be real sanitary, but this'll at least help slow the flow until we can break into that outpost and get some supplies. Your God better be watching out for us."

Gabriel smiled and began to pray. "Though I walk through the valley of the shadow of death..."

Chapter 25

Poe prowled around the circle of people that had formed in the market. Nervous whispers had taken on a cicada-like drone. The drone got louder when two men carried a shirtless, semi-conscious Garcia into the center or the circle and lashed his hands to a thick pole that had been installed for the occasion. Poe's face reddened, and his scowl lengthened as he watched.

"What are you doing," Doc whispered.

Poe ignored him and stepped toward the middle of the circle.

"Who doesn't remember the weeks and months immediately following the Impact? The riots. The looting. The murders in the street because of decades-old grudges. There was no law. Just chaos. Just anarchy." Poe walked to the other side of the circle and stopped, making eye contact with a few people. "Humans need organization. Humans need laws and people willing to enforce them. We saw what happened when there's no one to enforce laws. The days immediately following Impact showed us that. Fortunately, some of us were prepared. Many years before Impact we started making plans to bring civilization back to an uncivil world!"

A few people clapped. A murmur rolled like a wave around the circle.

"A few of us understood that a society without laws isn't a civilization at all." Poe glanced at Doc. "We created a system of currency, a form of taxation, a way to provide electricity, sometimes,"--the murmur rolled through the crowd again--"the ability to defend you from other tribes out there that want to hurt us and take what we've built here. And make no mistake about it, there are other tribes out there. Tribes, or groups, that are just as wild and lawless as those days after Impact. Animals. Bottom feeders. Hyenas. We protect you from that."

He strolled back to the other side of the circle looking around the ring.

"The rule of law is what sets us apart. And those laws apply to each and every one--"

"You steal our sons!" a man yelled from within the crowd. The murmur escalated to a dull rumble rolling around the ring.

"Who said that?"

Garcia stirred on the post. He lifted his head, then dropped it again.

Doc stepped forward and whispered in Poe's ear. "Don't do anything rash. This is volatile."

The crowd rustled around until a man stepped out into the ring. He looked like he was in his later thirties and wore overalls and a Chicago Cubs cap that was frayed along the bill. He crossed his arms over his chest, his feet planted shoulder-width apart.

"I did," he said. "Your speech here about law and civilization is bullshit."

"Don't," Doc said.

"Why do you say that?" Poe said, his voice reflecting the anger building inside him.

"You take our sons and hold them over us so that no one will oppose you." The man turned and looked at the crowd. "My son went. Then he was murdered in cold blood by one of your other men!" He turned back to face Poe again. "Shot in the back of the head! Guess what, you son-of-a-bitch you don't have him to hold over me anymore. I can oppose you. And there's a lot more of us."

Doc whispered in Poe's ear again.

Poe nodded. "Your son was Jordan Facione. I'm deeply sorry about the loss of your son. But he's the reason we're here," Poe said. He motioned to Garcia. "This is my son. He's the one accused of shooting your son."

"Accused?! What--"

"My son denied the charges. There are no witnesses to dispute his denial. But as a demonstration that no one is above the law, he is here to face justice for the accusations against him. He is to be whipped five times. Would you like to administer one of the lashes?"

The man charged.

Three Ravens immediately stepped in front of Poe and the man crashed into them. They pushed back, and he fell to the ground. More armed Ravens pushed through the crowd and created a barrier between the people and the center of the ring.

"You have to choose your battles, Harry," Doc said as quietly as he could. "This one is one you can't win. You have that guy killed, and you might fire up a full-bore revolution. It's not worth it."

Poe looked around the ring. Some people had begun to push at the Ravens standing guard. Others yelled things he couldn't make out over the cacophony. He unhooked his whip and cracked the air with it.

A hush fell over the ring except for Garcia who had begun to scream unintelligible words and try to push himself to his feet.

The whip cracked again, and a crimson streaked opened up on Garcia's back from his shoulder blade to his hip. He pushed up on one foot and his back arched. Another crack, another streak. Garcia screamed. The crowd was silent. Drops of blood pelted Poe as he pulled the whip back for another swing; this one cut deeper. Garcia's scream reverberated off the dilapidated buildings lining the street.

After the fifth one, Poe handed the whip to Doc and wiped his eyes. "Get the men to the boat. I've got some traitors to collect. They're the reason for all this. I listened to you and showed mercy with that guy, don't expect the same when I get them back here."

Chapter 26

Cain worked on changing Frank's bandages. His shoulder had gotten worse. The infection was spreading. Fast. Warm red streaks ran all the way to his elbow and down his ribcage almost to his waist. The putrid smell assaulted his nose, causing Cain to choke a little.

Frank had spent more time sleeping than normal the last day and a half. Since Taggart had drug Peters out and tied him to the tree, Frank was in the bed. He alternated between chills and dripping in sweat as the fever ravaged him.

"Cain, am I going to die?"

"No, we're gonna get through this. I'll figure something out, I promise. Our plan almost worked last time," Cain said, nodding toward the now boarded up hole they'd knocked in the wall. "Ten more minutes and we would've been three miles away."

You failed. Again. As soon as the time came to make the tough decision, you froze up.

Frank shivered and pulled away from Cain. He curled up in a trembling ball on the bed.

Cain looked out the window and chuckled. "Frank, you see your dog over there torturing Peters? C'me here. You want to see this."

Frank groaned but pushed himself to his feet and looked out the window. He laughed. Taggart had tied a rope around Peters's neck and tied the other end to the big tree like a dog on a tie-out. Maisey would come up to Peters and growl and snap at him until he was at the end of his rope and it choked him.

"Good girl, Maisey," Frank tried to yell, but his voice wasn't strong enough for her to hear him.

"Couldn't happen to a nicer asshole," Cain said.

Cain and Frank both turned and looked when they heard Taggart's heavy footsteps on the basement stairs. The deadbolts released, and the barrel of a handgun poked into the room. Taggart followed it in, exhaling a cloud of smoke.

"M'rnin' boys. Ravens 'r comin' ta pick ya up in a lil bit." He tossed a pile of clothes on the ground. "Fine somethin' in th're that fits 'n git it on. Cover up 'is nasty arm too. Don't w'nt the Ravens thinkin' I'm givin' 'em damaged goods."

Cain remained still. Frank bent to pick up the clothes, but Cain motioned for him to stop.

"We aren't doing it. You'll have to shoot us," Cain said.

Before Cain could react, the man had him by the hair and forced his chin up, holding the gun under it.

"Tough guy. Think I won't shoot ya?" He pulled the gun down and pushed it up against Frank's chin. "Maybe I'll do him 'stead."

Like she could sense it, Maisey came charging at the window. She stuck her snout through the bars next to Cain's head. She bared her teeth and snapped at the air. She didn't bark, but her growl came from somewhere deep and primal. Hate-filled. The skin on Cain's arms broke into goosebumps.

"You shoot us, you don't get paid, and you have the Ravens pissed off that you killed us before they could," Cain said.

"Easy, g'rl," the man said. His voice was less certain than Cain had ever heard it. He moved in slow motion, pulling the gun away from Frank and pointed it toward the dog. "Now take 'notha step at me, ya lil' bitch."

The steady hum of an engine punctuated with the thump of a boat cutting through small waves diffused the tension. The man stole a couple of quick glances out the window.

Maisey had stopped growling but held her stance and her focus on Taggart.

He kicked the pile of clothes. "Put 'em on!"

Cain stepped toward Taggart.

Maisey flinched and unleashed another long growl that hung in the thick air. Her back haunches coiled like a spring. Her front feet spread wide, ready to launch her forward. The fur on the scruff of her neck bristled.

Taggart glanced out the window again. His face reddened, and his mustache twitched under the cloud of cigarette smoke around him. With the speed of a rattlesnake strike, he pistol-whipped

Cain, catching him unprepared for the blow. Cain staggered then dropped to a knee.

"I said, get 'em on!"

The copper taste of his blood nauseated and infuriated Cain. He spat at the man's boots, then staggered to his feet, bracing himself against the wall. His vision in his right eye was already ringed in a reddish corona. Each pulse brought more heat and swelling to his face.

"Screw you," he said.

"Do it! 'Fore I kill bote ya." Taggart brought the gun back for another blow.

"Wait!" Frank yelled. "I'll put the clothes on." He bent and picked up a long sleeve denim shirt and slipped it on. He winced when the shirt brushed against the infected wound.

Cain sighed and picked up a shirt out of the pile. The red cloud in his right eye grew thicker by the minute. He knew his eye would be good and black. Hopefully, it would raise some red flags with the Ravens.

Voices grew louder outside the window. Cain froze. He knew two of the voices. One was Jovi. The other one was Poe! That was a voice he knew he wouldn't forget, ever. That day in the driveway played itself out over and over every time he shut his eyes, Poe's professorial tone tinged with arrogance, his smug confidence when he thought he was bullying a widow and teenage boys, the wide-eyed fear in his mother's eyes when she felt the pain of the bullets. Cain knew he'd never forget her face or his voice. The emotional look on Frank's face said that he recognized the voice too.

The bounty hunter yelled out the window that he was gathering the prisoners. He bound their hands with a couple of lashes of twine and marched them up the stairs and into the yard. He went to retrieve Peters from the tree. Maisey plodded over and stood by Frank, who reached down and scratched her head.

Poe smiled. Several teeth were missing; a few others were broken and jagged. His beard was shaved off, his glasses were gone, and he had what looked like blood smeared on his face. He was flanked by Jovi, and two other Ravens carrying rifles. Now, he looked the part of the ruthless killer he was.

"Well, well, well. It's my little orphan friends. I am terribly sorry about your mom."

Cain held his breath, hoping he wouldn't say anything else about their mom's death. He needed his wits about him and having to worry about Frank's reactions would be a distraction.

You don't want Frank to know who really killed his momma. As long as no one talks about it, it didn't happen, right?

The bounty hunter blew out a puff of smoke, then chomped on the end of his cigarette before speaking. "Dese boys you're lookin' fer?"

"Indeed, they are. What happened to the little one," Poe said spotting Cain's swollen purple eye. "You told me they were undamaged."

"Ya know, boys'll be boys. Dey got rastlin' round, one of 'em got a lil carried away." The bounty hunter nodded at Peters.

Poe shook his head. "This isn't what we agreed on. It's going to cost you. I'm lowering the agreed upon price by a third."

"A third! Dat's highway robb'ry! We had a deal...'less your word ain't w'rth nothin!"

Poe pulled a gun from a holster under his jacket. He aimed it at the bounty hunter. "I could kill you and just take them for free. Would that be a better alternative for you?"

The old man shook his head.

"That's settled then." He lowered the gun and turned toward his men. "These guys look familiar to you, Jovi?"

Jovi raised his eyes and met Cain's. He looked as scared as he had the day in the timber, maybe more so. His legs trembled a little, and his fingers lingered over the hilt of a hunting knife sheathed by his side.

"Yes, sir."

"Go ahead, tell them what happened because you failed to capture them." Poe's face reddened. His eyes moved back and forth between Cain and Jovi. Murderous rage seeped through the milky acid scarring. He'd gone from looking the part of the soulless killer to downright demonic in a matter of seconds.

"They killed my family. All of them. My mom. My dad. Dead. Because of you!" A single tear marched down his face.

Poe laughed. "Yes, you boys are all orphans now, and you all belong to me. Who's this?" He waved his gun toward Peters.

"Name's Brendan Peters. I'm the one that identified the brothers and alerted Mr. Taggart to their identities."

"Are you responsible for that shiner he has?"

Peters looked toward the old bounty hunter, then back at Poe. "Ya, he tried to escape. I stopped him. He deserves justice."

"Indeed he does," Poe smirked and looked toward the brothers. "You got kids, Mr. Peters?"

"Yes, a son. I'm looking forward to going home to him."

"What do you teach your son about respecting people's property?"

Peters shrugged.

"These boys belong to me. Do you know what happens when you hurt one of my boys?"

"I guess the bounty hunter there don't get as much--"

"Wrong! We play a game."

Cain's heart pounded. "Peters, shut the hell up. Don't say anything else!"

"The game's called you hurt mine, I kill yours. See you hurt one of my boys, so now I gotta kill one of yours. Or you."

"But--"

Poe pulled the trigger twice. Both shots struck Peters in the chest. His eyes fixed straight ahead; blood streamed from his lips. He fell face forward on the ground.

Cain's stomach lurched, but there was nothing in it to throw up. He hated Peters--and had tried to kill him a day ago--but the cold ease with which Poe had dispatched him was revolting.

Frank's fingers were intertwined, and he turned his thumbs over and over each other.

"It's okay, Frank. Stay calm. I'll figure something out, promise you," Cain whispered. Frank nodded without looking up from his hands.

"Back to business. Jovi, why don't you tell our friends again, what they cost you." Poe put his arm around Taggart's shoulder and said to him, "This should be good."

Now, Jovi's legs were both noticeably shaking. He met Cain's eyes again, this time they showed more than fear, they looked angry. Two more tears rolled downward.

"My family. They were butchered like that"--he motioned toward Peters's body--"after they were tortured."

Jovi stepped toward Cain, still shaking. He slammed his fist up and under Cain's ribcage, doubling him over. Cain gasped for breath.

Maisey barked and stepped forward a few steps.

"They killed... my...family," Jovi hissed between tears. He punched again, not as hard this time.

He bent down and hissed in Cain's ear.

"I should've listened to you. I should've run. They killed them anyway. Take this. Use it when you get a chance."

He forced something cold and metallic between Cain's bound hands.

"It's all your fault!" Jovi said. With his back still to Poe and Taggart, he straightened up and took a step back. "My family is dead!"

Cain, still doubled over and sucking for air, looked between his hands. It was a razor blade. The rising sun glimmered of its edge like a thin ray of hope. He manipulated it until he had it gripped between his fingertips, then he tried to stand up.

"Cain, you okay?" Frank asked.

"Yeah, I'll be okay."

"I stayed calm."

Cain smiled and looked at his brother. His big soulful eyes that longed for his younger brother's approval lit up when they saw the smile.

"You did good, Frank. Real good."

Cain's eyes met Jovi's again, the anger and fear were gone. Now he understood the rage he saw in them earlier wasn't directed at him, but toward the Ravens. The fear he saw was Jovi getting ready to betray them and sign his death sentence.

"Feel's good to be the stronger man, doesn't it, kid?" Poe said. "Now go get the boat ready.

There's another man back at Nevermore that I'm sure wants a piece of flesh from these two."

Jovi nodded, glanced at Cain, and walked down the hill toward the dock.

"What 'bout the boun'y on 'em?" Taggart said.

"Thought we discussed that earlier," Poe replied.

"Ya said you 'duced it, ne'er said how much you gonna pay."

Cain held his hands up against his stomach. With the blade between his ring finger and his little finger, he sliced through one of the three loops of twine around his wrists. He knew he had to be careful not to get seen, and not to cut all three so that the twine would fall to the ground.

Needing a diversion, he groaned, holding his side and dropped to one knee, shielding his wrists behind his leg. He sliced the second rope. Before he raised up, he eased the blade across the third, trying to cut only about halfway through so that he could easily tear it away when the time came. He felt the twine fall slack, then fall away from his wrists. He'd cut too deep!

It felt like it took the twine hours to fall to the ground. Every fraction of a second he watched in horror, praying that the argument held their attention. As soon as it hit the ground, he quickly covered the twine with his foot. He pretended to struggle to his feet, keeping his body turned as best he could to hide his bare wrists.

He thought it was possible to keep them from noticing for a few minutes. With the acid eyes,

Poe probably couldn't see that it was missing, and he didn't figure the old man would be looking too closely either. He prayed the other two were busy watching to see if their boss was going to kill the old man. He knew he only had a couple minutes at the most to figure out how to get Frank free and get away.

Jovi stood behind the wheel of the boat, its dual engines gently rumbling in the water. He held the bow in place with a rope looped around a post. The stern was still tied off with a loose knot. "She's ready," he yelled up the hill.

Poe reached out and took Frank's elbow and pushed him forward.

Maisey growled and advanced a couple of steps before halting and baring her teeth at Poe.

Finally, it clicked for Cain.

"Wait!" Cain screamed. "The bounty hunter's ripping you off. My brother's arm is infected. His shoulder. It's bad. Worse than my eye!"

"Don't know wha tha' boy talkin' bout. Look dat kid solid as an ox."

"Which side?" Poe demanded.

"The right."

Poe poked Frank's right shoulder with the gun barrel. Frank winced and backed away. He covered it with his bound hands.

Maisey barked and growled. It was the same hate-filled growl from before. This time it gave Cain hope instead of chills.

You're sacrificing something else that Frank loves to save yourself! You're pathetic! Nothing but a trail of dead bodies and scorched earth in your wake!

Poe holstered his gun and pulled out his hunting knife. He sliced open the arm of Frank's shirt, then tore it the rest of the way off. The skin around the bite mark glowed hot pink with a white center like a bullseye. Poe recoiled, then spun Frank around. The wound on his back was even worse.

Maisey barked and paced. With each step, she eased lower, and more of her teeth flashed in the sun.

"What the hell is this?" Poe demanded of the bounty hunter.

"Wha'?"

"This!" Poe yelled striking the wound hard with the barrel of the gun.

Frank cried out and tried to grab at his arm.

Maisey took two long strides forward and launched herself at Poe. He stumbled backward, and they both crashed to the ground. He wasn't able to get the knife pulled before she was on him again, snarling and snapping. That demonic growl sounded like it came from all around them. She forced her teeth close to his throat. He grunted and pushed her away with a forearm, but she bit down on it, drawing blood.

The two Ravens were slow to react, and they lunged to help Poe. One swung the stock of his rifle at the ravenous dog.

Cain ran to Frank and cut him free. He grabbed Frank's hand and pulled.

"Let's go!"

Frank resisted. "But--"

Jovi revved the engine in the boat.

"Now!"

Cain tugged his arm, not caring if it was the bad one or not. Frank followed and ran toward the boat, right on Cain's heels. He glanced back to see the bounty hunter and the Ravens all fighting to get Maisey off of Poe's arm.

Maisey's snarls and Poe's screams filled the air. A gunshot rang out. A yelp and a whimper followed. Another shot. A little fountain of water popped up where the bullet hit the lake.

Frank cried out for her but kept running.

Jovi revved the engine again. "Undo that last rope!" he yelled to Cain as the brothers reached the dock.

Frank tumbled aboard. Another shot rang out and struck the dock not five feet away from where Frank had just been. Cain got the rope free and lunged for the boat. Frank grabbed his hand and pulled him aboard as another bullet whizzed by.

Jovi gunned the engine. The bow rose up out of the water as he spun away from the dock.

The windshield exploded in a web of cracks.

"Go! Go! Go!" Cain yelled.

"That was close," Jovi muttered, banking the boat hard to the right.

Frank turned and saw Poe's men rumbling down the hill, lining up another shot. He pushed Cain to the floor and pressed himself against Jovi's back, his hands extended to the shattered windshield.

Jovi swung the boat back the other direction and buried the throttle.

Cain saw Frank's body jerk. Then a second time. And a third. He slid off Jovi and landed half on the other seat and half on the floor. Blood trickled from his mouth, and his eyes were wide.

"Frank! No!!"

Jovi banked the boat around the bend out of the line of fire then dropped off the throttle.

"No, keep going. We gotta get him to a doctor," Cain said to Jovi. "Frank! Stay with me, man." Cain couldn't hold back the tears. "Frank!"

Jovi gunned the engine again. The bow rose up then settled on plane as they thumped over the little waves.

"Hi Momma," Frank said, his voice barely more than a whisper. A smile crept across his face; his teeth were nearly invisible behind the blood trickling from his mouth.

"Frank, it's not Momma. It's me!"

"I missed you, Momma. I took care of Cain, I did. I took care of him."

Cain lifted Frank's head up so that he was right in front of his face. "Frank! Look at me! You're gonna be fine."

"Cain?" Frank said, his eyes searching, but not seeing his brother a foot in front of his face. "Cain!"

"Frank, I'm here! I'm here, buddy."

Frank smiled again. "Cain, Momma said"--he gasped for air--"she's proud of me."

Cain's sobs intensified. "I'm proud of you too, brother."

"Cain, Momma says it's okay. She"--gasp--"knows it was an accident, and you were"--gasp--"trying to save me."

Frank's eyes found his younger brother. He smiled again. He reached up and touched Cain's face. His fingers lingered for a long time on Cain's swollen eye. Cain forced a smile, too.

"I'm coming, Momma," Frank said. He took a long breath, then his eyes fixed straight ahead, and he slumped back. Cain felt for a pulse, but there wasn't any.

"No! Frank! Stay with me! I need you!"

Cain held Frank's body on his lap for a few minutes. Then he laid his brother out on the floor and shut his eyes. Cain sat there next to him as the boat bounced over the little waves. Finally, he pulled his legs up to his chest and rocked back and forth, repeating Frank's name over and over.

Chapter 27

Cain looked up as the boat swung in a wide curve and the engines revved down. So many houses lined the lakefront. Almost all of which probably sat empty since their owners died. Seeing all the lifeless homes lining the shore like grave markers in a cemetery, Cain shuddered. So much suffering. So much death.

And think of all the death that you're personally responsible for.

Jovi coasted toward a dock, when they got close he gunned one of the engines, spinning the boat. It kissed gently off the side of the dock. He tossed a rope over a post, pulled it snug, and tied it off.

"Hey, I'm really sorry about your brother. He saved our lives. We're gonna get his for him."

Cain looked up but couldn't speak. He wiped at his eyes and flinched when he pressed against his shiner.

"If you lift up that bench seat, there's handguns and rifles in there. Grab those bungee cords out of there too. And a couple flares."

Cain sat there, unable to move his eyes from Frank's lifeless body.

Yep, that one's on you too.

Jovi put his hand on Cain's shoulder. "C'mon. We're gonna kill that mofo, but we gotta get to moving."

Cain knew he had to go. He remembered how Frank had wanted to stay and hold their mom, but he made him leave her. Cain spoke; Frank listened, even though his guts must have been getting ripped out. Now he understood how hard that must've been for Frank to do. Now he respected Frank's ability to do it so much more.

"As soon as I heard Poe was coming to pick you guys up, I volunteered to come. Then I started planning how to kill him," Jovi said, as Cain began handing guns and supplies to him.

"How are we going to kill him here?" Cain said.

"Not here. He's heading to Usher Outpost. But he's got to drive all the way around the lake. We're only three miles away. And Scarlett's there."

"Scarlett?"

"Yeah. That's what they call the truck with the .50 caliber gun mounted on the back. We're going to beat him to it, take out the guards, and wait for him to show up. Grab that gas can over there, will ya?"

"I can't just leave him here," Cain said, again remembering not so many days ago when Frank had said the same thing to him.

You were running. Run and hide. It's one of the few things you're good at.

"We're not. We're gonna bury him in the lake," Jovi said. He used the bungee cords to strap the gas can to the swim ladder and started the engines. "Okay, I'll give you a minute to say goodbye, then we're going to open the gas can so it spills out, hit the throttle and let her head toward the middle of the lake. Then we'll light the gas. I know he deserves better, but under the circumstances, it's the best burial we can do."

A few minutes later they stood on the dock and watched the boat burn.

"We'll be together soon, Frank," Cain said, unable to look at the burning boat any longer.

Chapter 28

On the short ride to the outpost, Jovi explained about how he'd said he needed to be alone and needed to leave Nevermore for a ride. The Ravens allowed it because of what had happened with Garcia and his parents. He rode out past the outpost scouting places to bring the boat in and made sure that there was a vehicle there that would start. He told Cain that he thought Garcia would be with Poe and why he wasn't. Cain nodded every so often but wasn't absorbing most of what he was hearing.

"Okay, the outpost is just ahead," Jovi said. "We're going to go up in those woods and come at it from the back. It's just a guard post and roadblock since this is a main road into town. Usually, there are only a few guys out here at any given time. With Scarlett here, might be a few more. But, at most I would expect to see two at the back door. Most will be up front with the technical."

"Technical?"

"The truck with the cannon. Sometimes they also call it a gunship, or gunboat. We'll take out the guards, get inside, and then find our way to the roof. From there we'll have cover and the high ground and can take out the rest of them. Then we'll have that gun ready, so it's the last thing Poe sees when he drives up. Seems simple enough, right?"

You should tell him that anyone around you ends up dead. You should tell him not to get in a situation where his life depends on you, 'cuz you'll just stay hidden like you did with Gordon.

They slipped into the woods and to the top of a ridge. The peered over the top at the outpost fifty yards or so below. The outpost was an old elementary school laid out in almost a U shape around a central courtyard. The windows in many of the rooms had been painted over. Years worth of colorful graffiti adorned the walls.

The two long wings of the school had slanted roofs, but the middle section was flat, and Cain could see how it would be a prime spot to attack from. Three feet of brick rose above the floor that would provide cover but still enable a full range of firing down into the courtyard.

The Ravens would have some cover, though. A bell tower stood in the center courtyard. It was supported by four wide brick pillars with a spiral staircase twisting up the middle. The top of it was enclosed save for an opening on each side. Its bell had fallen and lie askew almost completely blocking one of the openings.

Jovi pointed toward the back of the school. One guard leaned against the wall near the door and smoked a cigarette; another stood a few feet away taking a leak on the side of the building. Cain and Jovi eased their rifles up and steadied them.

"I got smoker, you got pisser," Jovi said. "On the count of three."

"Yep."

"Ready. One. Two."

Two snaps echoed through the trees. Both Ravens dropped. Smoker writhed on the ground. Another snap, and he went still.

"What the--"

Breathing fast, Jovi rolled over. "I almost got us killed."

"I didn't fire. Where'd that come from?" Cain said.

"I don't know but whoever did it had a suppressor on the gun. That's why it sounded like a stick breaking and not a gunshot. I didn't have suppressors on these. If we'd fired these, half of Lake County would still be hearing the echoes from the shots. They'd have rolled that beast back here and lit us up."

"Well, we didn't. Frank must be watching out for us."

Jovi rolled back over and joined Cain. They watched a man in camouflage pants and a safari hat with grass sticking out of it helping a bloody man with long gray hair down out of the woods. Cain felt his heart lighten. Gabriel! He didn't know who the other man was but he was wearing the upside-down flag, so that was a good sign.

Cain scrambled up out of the grass; Jovi pulled him back down.

"What're you doing?"

"They're resistance. I know one of them. The other one's shirt. Upside-down flag. It's what the resistance wears."

Cain couldn't remember the last time he was so happy to see another person. He was probably closer to Gabriel that anybody since his dad died. When he was frustrated, Gabriel would listen and advise him. When he needed help, Gabriel would teach him. When he flipped Noah Meyer and shot him in the shoulder as a cover, Gabriel was there to celebrate his success.

"You said we were gonna take out the guards and make our way to the roof. It's this way. And we have reinforcements. Let's go," Cain said.

The crept down the hill. Cain carried his pistol and had the rifle slung across his back. Jovi carried his rifle in firing position. They heard a voice coming around the side of the building, and both dropped to the ground.

"Shit," Cain whispered.

A Raven walked toward them along the side of the building. Jovi aimed his rifle. The guy glanced up at the tree line as he walked.

"If he rounds the corner, I gotta take the shot. Then all hell's gonna break loose," Jovi said.

The man kept coming toward them, now just a few feet from the corner where he'd be able to see the bodies around back.

Cain held his breath but could hear Jovi's breath coming fast and shallow; his finger caressed the trigger.

The man stopped and looked around, then turned back the other direction.

Cain breathed and dropped his face into the dirt. Jovi did the same.

Once the man had gone around the front corner, the boys sprung up and ran to the back of the building. Cain lifted another handgun and a knife off of Pisser as the moved past him.

The door was a thick metal fire door. Jovi eased it open, and Cain rolled around it, pistol ready. Jovi followed him into the building and pulled the door shut behind them. Just inside the door, two dust-covered brooms leaned against the empty coat rack. Cain grabbed one of the brooms and threaded the thick wooden dowel through the door handles using the metal jamb between them for leverage.

"Won't hold for very long, but might buy us a minute or two if needed," he said and shrugged.

The two boys moved down the hall, back-to-back, guns facing outward and ready to fire. They passed an old classroom. The door was still propped open, and the bulletin board still had student art projects hanging from it. The ten-foot-long alphabet poster had fallen at one end and draped onto the floor.

They froze as they heard voices from the next room.

Jovi nodded to keep going. Cain shook his head.

"That might be where Gabriel is," Cain whispered.

"It's locked. See the key on the wall next to it." He paused and motioned for Cain to go into the empty classroom. Once there he said, "There are prisoners here. They were going to keep you and your brother here with them. That must be where they are."

"Well let's go get 'em out."

They decided on a plan and crept back into the hall. Jovi eased the key off the wall and positioned it by the lock. He nodded at Cain. Cain nodded back. Jovi unlocked the door and flung it open. Cain barged through the door, gun drawn.

He focused on a set of sapphire blue eyes staring back at him. Frank's eyes.

Chapter 29

"Skinny C... Cain?" Gordon said.

"Gordon? Gordon!." Cain lowered his gun and rushed to embrace his old friend. Tears rolled down his face. He didn't know if it was actual joy from seeing him or because of his resemblance to Frank. Either way, Cain couldn't stop the tears. "My mom told me you escaped, but I didn't believe her."

"I did. Then I w.. w... went back to try to h... help other boys escape. They c... c... caught us and put us he... he... here." He nodded toward an older boy seated on a low bookcase.

The other guy looked more like he escaped from a Revenge of the Nerds movie rather than the farm. He was long and thin, like a pencil, and wore glasses that had thick, horn-rimmed frames and lenses that had to be a half-inch thick. His hair was straight and blonde, and his bangs hung in a straight line covering most of his eyebrows.

He hopped off the bookcase and strode over holding his hand to Cain. "So, you're the infamous Skinny Cain. John McCoy, good to meet you. You've stirred up a hell of a shit storm."

Cain shook his hand. "You don't look like the type they normally send to the farms."

"You don't look like some seditionist leader, either." McCoy smiled. "I'm not from the farms. I was Raven. Full-patched member and everything. They stripped my jacket and sent me to the farm to cover up for that psycho, Garcia. Gordon helped me get away."

Cain glanced at Jovi; he raised his eyebrows and tilted his head as if to say 'I don't know.' Even if this guy was only on the farm for a few days, he had plenty of reasons to turn on the Ravens. But with true believers, the loyalty ran much deeper, and its pull was stronger. The way he said 'full-patched member' sounded like pride to Cain. Old habits died hard, and this guy's nonchalant air reminded Cain too much of how Peters acted.

Jovi cracked open the door and peered down the hall. "Shit! Poe's already here."

"What? How? You said it would take him an hour."

"Yeah. We took the boat. He'd have had to go by land and drive all the way around the--"

"Taggart had a boat. The bounty hunter. He had a fishing boat."

"Shit!" Jovi punched the air. "Well two of us could've taken out four in a surprise attack. But now we're screwed."

Cain paced back and forth, then stopped. "Gabriel. He's in here somewhere. They were armed. That gives us four. Or maybe just three depending on how badly he's hurt."

"Got a gun? I'm in. That gives us five," John said.

Cain shot a look to Jovi again without getting a response. He pulled out the pistol he'd taken from the dead Raven and gave it to Gordon. He hesitated, then unslung the rifle from his back and handed it to John.

That was dumb. He's Raven. 'Full-patched member.' He's gonna kill you with that gun.

As if reading his mind, Jovi nodded at John and said, "You shoot him with that he's going to kill you."

"We're gonna have to split up to try to find them," Cain said. He turned to John. "We're looking for a guy with long gray hair. He's bloody and with a guy wearing a shirt with an American flag upside-down. Gordon, you come with me. We'll head to the second floor. Jovi, you take the left side, John you got the right. When someone finds them, head to the roof. If you don't find them meet on the roof in fifteen."

"Don't shoot unless you have no choice," Jovi said. "Once the shooting starts, we're all in. We're either going to kill all of them, or we're all gonna die. I'd rather skew the odds in our favor with some surprise shots."

They cracked the door open. No Ravens. They slipped out and dispersed in their different directions. Cain and Gordon spun around the corner. Cain checked the stairs. Empty. They climbed them and peeked around the corner. They were in the middle of the long hallway. Cain motioned for Gordon to follow and eased out into the hall. It seemed impossibly long and open. He felt even more exposed than when he was trying to run across the road when they were trying to escape from their home.

He heard voices. Poe was one of them!

The pair ducked out of the hall into an alcove outside of a girls' bathroom. Half of a smashed water fountain hung on the wall; above it was a broken mirror. They squatted down in the shadows. Cain watched in the mirror. Poe was talking to the two men with him at Taggart's. Anger, hatred, roiled his gut. His heart pounded in his chest. He wanted to take the shot. He wanted to kill the bastard, but knew he'd be signing everyone else's death sentences.

Since when has that ever stopped you before? Your hands got lots of blood on 'em.

The trio turned off into a doorway at the far end of the hall. Cain took a deep breath, then darted across the hall, Gordon right behind him. He checked a door. Locked. He moved to the next one. The handle turned, and he barged into the room. Empty.

"Damn,"

He could still hear the Raven and Poe talking down the hall, and motioned to Gordon that they were going across the hall to check the last door in this direction. The older boy nodded. They rushed across. The door was unlocked, and they burst in.

Gabriel was sitting on a teacher desk while the other man closed his wound with some crude stitches.

"Gabriel!" He hurried to the older man's side.

"Cain! You're still alive!" Gabriel's face showed his emotion. His eyes squinted, and his voice cracked. He turned his head toward the sky. "Thank you, God. Thank you."

Gordon stood at the door and watched down the hall.

"They haven't killed me yet. What are you doing here?"

Only because people keep dying for you.

"We've got two rockets. We were gonna take out that truck. They shot up our truck. Killed Brian Morrow. We got away, but shrapnel of some kind got me."

"Cain! They're c... c... coming this way," Gordon said in a loud whisper.

"I've got other guys with me. They're headed to the roof. Gonna make a stand, and hopefully get a couple of 'em with a surprise shot. Let's get up there. We'll get the men. You get the truck."

"N... no time. They're t... two doors away. You g... go. I'll distract th... them."

With that, Gordon swung the door open and charged down the hall.

More blood spilled to save your ass.

Cain hurried to the door and peeked out. Gordon slammed into the Ravens. At first, he managed to push his way through, then they recovered and dove on top of him. His face crashed into the tile floor.

"Where did you-- Hey, he's got the brand. Is this the prisoner that escaped the farm?"

You're really going to stand here while they drag him away... again? He won't survive this time. He just sacrificed himself for you! Worthless! You're worthless!

One Raven knelt with his knee on the back of Gordon's neck. The other radioed men downstairs to check the prisoner. When the reply came that the prisoners were gone, they pulled Gordon to his feet.

"Back to your cell, buddy. Nice try though," one said.

With one holding a gun on each side of him, they escorted him down the hall and around the corner. Before he disappeared, Gordon turned and looked down the hall. Cain met his sapphire blue eyes. Frank's eyes.

Frank's words filled his head. 'I took care of Cain, I did. I took care of him... Cain, Momma said she's proud of me.'

Cain motioned for Gabriel and the other man to slide behind him and head toward the stairs.

You did it again, you coward.

"Go! Go!" Cain urged them. "I gotta go get Gordon back."

He sprinted down the hall. He ran past the stairs that they'd come up. Past the closed doors and the bathroom alcove. As he was going to round the corner that they'd turned with Gordon, Poe stepped out of a room. Before he could react, Poe swung a knife. It bit into his hand. The gun slipped from his grasp. He dove for it, but Poe was too quick and kicked it away. He landed hard on the floor. Poe tried to kick him, but he rolled away and scrambled to his feet.

His heart felt like it was going to come out of his chest. He pulled the knife that he'd taken off the dead Raven. Poe leered, and bent forward, his arms curved out like an Old West cowboy waiting to draw his guns. He stepped to the side; Cain followed suit.

"Skinny Cain. Your dad said you were tough. I have to admit, I underestimated you."

They each kept stepping as they circled and studied each other with the intensity of two prizefighters waiting for the other one to make a mistake.

"Don't talk about my dad."

"Your dad was one of us. You're one of us. Did you know that? He was one of my best friends. He was like a brother to me."

"You don't know my dad."

Cain faked a lunge. Poe parried to the right and winced just a little bit. But it was enough.

"Allan Coldrake. He helped us start the Ravens after Impact."

"You're lying."

Cain knew his dad was an abusive drunk, certainly not a good guy, but a Raven? No way.

They circled again. Cain's back was to the open door that Poe had emerged from. He backed slowly into the room.

"You could come be one of us. Your dad would be proud. I could use a smart kid like you."

Cain reached back with his bleeding hand, grasped a student desk and threw it toward Poe. Poe avoided it, but let out an audible gasp.

"Your ribs hurt where I beat you with your own baton? Hurt your pride a little to be bested by a kid?"

Poe's face reddened. Grimacing, he faked a lunge.

Yelling started outside, below the windows. Someone had discovered the bodies. Poe glanced toward the window. Cain grabbed another desk and tossed toward him. It tumbled and slid across the tile. Poe stopped it with his foot, gasping again, then pushed it back toward Cain.

Cain watched it slide toward him. When it was close enough, he planted his foot on it and launched himself into the air. He caught Poe momentarily distracted by the commotion outside. The blade caught Poe's cheek and sliced it open. Cain rolled on the ground and got to his feet, backing toward the door.

Poe lumbered forward, blood gushing from his face. He swiped at Cain but missed. Cain sprung forward aiming for Poe's stomach, but missed and stuck the knife deep into his leg. Poe fell forward, landing on the knife and pushing it deeper.

Cain tried to pry Poe's knife away, but he was able to hold on. He stabbed with it and cut Cain's shoulder.

The first shot echoed through the halls.

"Shit!"

Cain ran out the door, searching for the gun. He snatched it up and ran the direction they'd gone with Gordon. Around the next corner was another set of stairs. Two Ravens were headed up them. Cain fired and ducked around the wall.

"What the! Man down! Man down!"

Cain rolled around the wall and looked over the railing. He fired another shot. Missed. But the Raven dove away. Cain ran down four steps and looked again. The Raven was just rolling out from behind the wall. A bullet shattered the window behind him, sending a waterfall of glass to the concrete below.

Cain fired. A chunk of the corner exploded next to the guy's shoulder. The Raven rolled out again, but before he could shoot his body was rocked by gunfire, and he fell to the floor. Blood spread out in a pool around him.

Cain ran down the steps two at a time. He skidded to a stop next to the dead Ravens. No one in the hall. He looked the other way. There they were.

The two Ravens with Gordon were headed toward the door to the outside. One turned and spotted him. He let go of Gordon and motioned for the other guy to get the prisoner out. Cain fired. Tile broke and crashed to the ground where the bullet hit the wall.

RAT-Tat-Tat-Tat-Tat

The Raven opened fire. Bullets ate at the corner to his right. Tiles cracked and fell. Dust billowed.

RAT-Tat-Tat

Cain rolled out, partially concealed in the dust, and fired three times. Two of them struck home; a crimson mist permeated the dust. He ran forward, grabbed the dead man's rifle and charged into the courtyard. The sudden bright light forced him to squint.

After his eyes adjusted, he saw John McCoy slumped against the wall, his eyes blank and fixed straight ahead. McCoy must have been the who had saved him on the stairs. Cain bent and closed his eyes. His gun was missing, but Cain snatched the knife and shoved it into the empty sheath still strapped to his belt.

He heard fire coming from the roof. A lot of it. Ravens returned fire from the courtyard. He was surprised to see Gabriel's partner sprinting up the spiral staircase of the bell tower. About mid-way up, he fell, blood pouring between the wrought-iron steps.

He spotted Gordon and a Raven about twenty-five feet ahead. They were struggling as Gordon tried to pull himself free. The Raven swept Gordon's leg pulling them both to the ground.

Cain charged ahead. Bullets ricocheted off the concrete to his left. The Raven rolled over, pinning Gordon under him. Cain tossed the gun aside, pulled the knife, and jumped, planting it in the Raven's back. Cain grabbed him by the hair.

He pulled the knife out and slid it across the guy's throat, then threw his body to the ground.

Gordon pushed himself up. Cain grabbed the gun and ran to take cover behind one of the brick pillars supporting the bell tower. The resistance man was pulling himself up the stairs.

"Go!" he said to Gordon. "Get to cover. Or the roof."

Gordon sprinted toward the building, zig-zagging to avoid the gunfire around him.

Cain moved toward the spiral stairs.

Bullets pinged off the metal. He rose up and fired the assault rifle. It recoiled more than he was expecting and he nearly dropped it. He ducked back down, got his bearings and rose up again. He fired, but missed, distracted by Poe being helped out of the school from another door.

The metal vibrated with impacts. He didn't duck and opened fire on Poe and the men helping him. Brick exploded next to him. He ducked. Then leaned around the other side of the pillar and unleashed a torrent of fire that ripped into the nearest Raven.

They were getting close to getting Poe to the truck. He tried to fire, but the magazine was empty. He glanced around and realized why the man was trying to get up the stairs. From the roof, the tower blocked his ability to get a clear shot at the gunship. The top of the tower would give him cover and an unobstructed view.

He sprinted up the stairs. A ricochet sparked right in front of him. He reached the man, who had almost clawed his way to the top. Cain grabbed him by the shirt and pulled him the rest of the way. He collapsed behind the safety of the brick walls.

"Take it... out," the man said, the blood in his mouth starting to garble his words.

The truck engine roared to life.

The man handed Cain the rocket launcher. "It's ready. Just aim... and fire. You won't miss."

Cain stood in the opening and rested the launcher on his shoulder. "It's Skinny Cain. In the tower!" one of them yelled. Bullets whizzed around him. He ducked.

Chicken shit! This is your chance!

He raised back up and tried to aim but couldn't get a good look.

Poe pushed one of the men out of the way and pulled himself up on the .50 caliber gun.

The truck tires spun, then grabbed, and it lurched forward.

Worthless. Gutless.

Cain stepped up on a pile of bricks and balanced the launcher on his shoulder and the fallen bell.

Poe sneered. Blood dripped from his mouth. He pointed the gun at Cain.

Cain saw the black depth of the massive barrel.

THUNK... THUNK... THUNK... THUNK

Poe screamed as the vibration rattled his ribs, throwing his aim off.

Dull thuds as the shots pounded into the cast iron bell.

Cain took a breath and pulled the trigger.

The tower filled with smoke, but it didn't obscure his vision of the orange fireball that rolled skyward when the rocket struck home.

Cain's legs gave out, and he collapsed in a heap next to the resistance fighter.

"You did good, kid," the man said before his eyes closed and his head dropped.

Cain didn't know how long he sat there listening to the crackle of the burning truck. But it was the sweetest sound he'd heard in a long time.

"I got him for you, Frank."

Chapter 30

Cain opened his eyes to snoring louder than a freight train. He sat up in bed, looking around the room for Frank, praying it had all been a dream.

Frank wasn't there. And he wasn't in his bedroom. Jovi snored away, stretched out on a beat-up sofa across the room. Dust in the air mixed with the light streaming through the windows to cast almost a heavenly spotlight on a man with long gray hair that held a walking stick in one hand and a drink in the other. He smiled when he saw Cain stirring.

"How you feeling, Cain?" he said. "Do you remember much?"

Cain did but didn't want to. He was alone. No family. Anyone close to him ended up dead. The guilt and emptiness made him want to just lie back down and never wake up.

He nodded because he didn't want to talk about it.

Gabriel smiled and raised his glass. "I'd offer you one, but you're underage, and you know, laws are what separates us from the animals. I think I already did my penance for this one."

Jovi stirred on the couch. He stretched and sat up. A smile crossed his fuzzy face. His beard looked like it had actually started to grow in, or maybe it was just the lighting.

"You boys did amazing things. God is indeed great. Now comes the hard part. Ravens are on the ropes, we have to convince people to revolt," Gabriel said, sipping his drink. "We can do it. They'll follow you."

Cain flopped back down on the bed.

"My sister is out there somewhere," Jovi said. "I've got to find her, and then I'm going to kill Garcia."

"If people rebel, we might be able to have a transition of power without much bloodshed."

"Without much bloodshed? I think there's been plenty of bloodshed already. And I plan on there being one more," Jovi said, the grief coming out in his voice. "Poe is alive. If they realize you have him, they're going to send everybody and their mother at you. You think there won't be much bloodshed?"

Cain bolted up in bed. "Poe's alive?"

Gabriel shot a frown at Jovi. "Yes. He survived the explosion. He's burned pretty badly, though. We have him under guard at the church. We've got a doctor that's treating him."

"What in the hell are you keeping him alive for?" Cain yelled.

"He's valuable. He can be a negotiation chip."

Cain flopped back down on the bed. A negotiation chip? That man was responsible for the death of most of his family. He needed to die, not get traded back to his people. Poe's words felt like a pillow, suffocating him. 'He was one of my best friends. He was like a brother to me.' Acid roiled in his stomach. He forced it down, but hate replaced it.

You can kill him.

"Gabriel, can you give Jovi and me a few minutes?"

Gabriel hesitated, then nodded and left, closing the door behind him.

"What's your plan?" Cain asked.

Jovi shrugged. "Don't really know. I just know I've got to be the one to see the life drain out of the motherfucker's eyes. You've got some skin in this too. You want to come?"

"But you've got no plan. No idea how to get to Garcia or where your sister is? Sounds like a suicide mission."

Jovi's eyes met Cain's. They burned with hatred and sorrow. Cain understood the feeling.

"If it's a suicide mission, well, I can think of less epic ways to die."

* * *

Cain eased into the room, not exactly sure what to expect. A single lightbulb burned dimly overhead illuminating a crucifix on the wall but not much else. He could hear the generator chugging away outside, making sure the power stayed even. An IV bag hung above a man in a hospital bed. Another monitor provided a slow and steady metallic heartbeat.

Cain approached him. Wrapped in only a sheet, attached to several medical machines, Poe didn't look nearly as fearsome. Bandages covered most of his face and shoulders. He actually looked small and frail lying there, dependent on the machines to keep him alive.

Cain fingered the IV bag, then slowly ran his finger across the heart monitor.

You can do it. You want to do it. End him!

Cain eyed the electrical outlet that powered the machines. He glanced back toward the door where Jovi stood. His friend nodded.

Poe's eyes blinked open. Despite his weak appearance, Cain felt a wave of hatred pour over him. It made him feel strong. He leaned over Poe's bed.

"So, you... come here too... kill me," Poe's voice was raspy and weak.

"I'd like nothing more."

"What's... stopping you then?"

"I didn't come here to kill you. Although for a split-second I wanted to."

Poe wheezed.

"I came here so we could play a game. I'm not sure what it's called, but it goes like this: you kill mine, now I kill yours. That's right, Poe. We're going to kill your son."

Author's note

I hope you enjoyed reading Scorched Earth. Be sure to look for Book Two: Tribes, available Fall 2018.

Also, please take a few moments to write a short review of the book. I appreciate the feedback.

Made in the USA
Columbia, SC
22 December 2017